Clearcut Danger

Lesley Choyce

Formac Publishing Company Limited
Halifax, Nova Scotia 1992

Cover: Rick Paine

Canadian Cataloguing in Publication Data

Choyce, Lesley, 1951-
Clearcut danger

ISBN 0-88780-338-5(pbk)
ISBN 0-88780-214-1(board)

I. Title.

PS8555.H668C4 1995   jC813'.54   C95-950273-4
PZ7.C46C1   1995

Formac Publishing Company Limited
5502 Atlantic Street
Halifax, Nova Scotia B3H 1G4

Printed and bound in Canada

Contents

1	Shooting Geese	1
2	A Hero's Secret	7
3	Public Euphoria	12
4	Indian Names	20
5	Against the Entire Town	26
6	Two's Company	33
7	Inside the Pulp Mill	39
8	Uncle George — Medicine Man	44
9	Worried Parents	48
10	Just Say No!	55
11	Invasion Begun	60
12	A Done Deal	67
13	Looking for Help	71
14	Mrs. Deveau Plays by the Rules	78
15	Sludge Quotient Versus Pure Water	83
16	Looking for Allies	89
17	What the Osprey Knows	95
18	Help from Greenpeace	103
19	Night Shadows	108
20	Clearcut Confrontation	114
21	A Question of Ownership	121
22	Back Cove's Secrets	126

Chapter One

Shooting Geese

It had been a bad day at school. In my Contemporary World Issues class, Mr. Eisner got us talking about how the new pulp mill was finally going to bring our town, East Harbour, into the twentieth century. Everybody thought it sounded great, including me. Alana, my girlfriend, was the one to say that it might not all be good. She said she wasn't sure she wanted any big changes. She likes East Harbour just the way it is. And if that wasn't enough, she added, "A pulp mill could really do some damage to the environment."

Man, you should have heard the guys give her a hard time over that one. "Just the way it is, are you crazy or what?" Robbie Robicheau said. I knew what he was thinking. I hear it all the time. *This place is boring. This town sucks.* So if you put in a new mill, the guys can drop out of school, get a job making good money, and never look back. Just put your brain in park and have it easy for the rest of your born days.

I was a little confused by what Alana said but then a lot about her baffles me.

"Why didn't you say something?" she asked me in the hallway.

"I was going to, but the bell rang. I didn't have a chance," I told her. I was lying. In truth, I was thinking I might be lucky enough to end up at the mill

1

myself. Then I wouldn't have to move away to get a good job.

"Sure," she said and walked away.

The girl can be moody. But she wasn't really mad at me, I knew that. We've been together since grade nine. We're pretty different, but ever since I first met her I've been crazy about her. She has all these strong opinions and always says what's on her mind. Sometimes she gets ticked off because it takes me a little longer to catch on. So if I'm just sitting there in Eisner's class trying to figure out what she's saying … well, sometimes Alana thinks I just want to go along with the other guys, that I'm afraid to think for myself. But it's not like that at all.

So I didn't try to explain it to her. Rather than get into an argument, I thought we should give each other a little breathing room. After school, instead of going over to her house, I decided to escape from civilization for a little while. I took off for a hike down the harbour to Back Cove.

Man, I love winter. I jogged for a while along the shore until I got to the cove. There it was. My place. Not a soul around. White ice. Deep, dark green spruce trees on both sides. I stopped and just spaced out, standing there sucking in clean air, watching puffy little clouds of breath come out of my mouth.

Winter made it easier to get out here. The frozen ice along the edge of the harbour was just like my own highway to heaven. I started walking again just as a light snow began falling. The sky was getting darker. Pretty soon it would be pitch black but I didn't want to rush home. I couldn't get lost out here, and I needed this, just me and the cove. I wished now that I had brought Alana along. She was on this kick of talking about "her people," as she called them. Her Micmac ancestors. She'd say that they saw the natural world as being sacred ... the trees, the sky, the water, everything. I can relate to that. I don't know if I'd use the word *sacred*, but I do know how I feel when I'm out here alone. How to explain it? I feel okay. I feel right. As if all the stuff that's screwed up doesn't matter. It's kind of like being cured.

So I was just hiking along, spacing out, and I rounded a little outcropping of rocks and saw a skidoo parked on the ice. I'd never seen this one before. Man, what a machine. It looked like it had plenty of muscle and this thing must have been brand new. Who around here could afford one like that, I wondered.

Then I saw a guy in a hunter's jacket walking up the shoreline on the other side of Back Cove. I knew immediately that it was Tom Murray, the man with all the promises. He was the spokesman for Alliance Limited, the company that was going to build the mill and bring East Harbour into the twentieth century. Tom was always smiling and everybody liked him. I guess good old Tom was just out to shoot himself a couple of birds for supper. Nothing wrong with that.

Murray had the town eating out his hand, and here he was out for a little sport.

I saw what he was after. Out on the ice, near the open water, were maybe thirty Canada geese, just sitting there. Yeah, Murray had a shotgun. He was going in for the kill. It was getting dark so the guy was going to have it easy.

I do some hunting myself, and I was wishing I was out there with Tom and a gun of my own. I sure didn't mind the idea of a feed of fresh cooked goose meat. Murray is a guy with lots of money. He's one of those types who come from away and hunt for sport. Still, I kind of wondered what it would be like to be in his shoes. He probably had a top-of-the-line shotgun and never blinked twice at the price tag on that major skidoo he had parked there.

Then I heard the first blast of the gun. And the second. Then there was a pause, and I heard a third blast, a fourth. Another pause as the gunshot echoed off the ice. When I heard the fifth and sixth shots I decided to get down there and check things out. I could barely make him out in the distance. I guess he was reloading. And then he fired again into the flock as they flapped their wings on the water in panic and confusion trying to get away. They were too far from shore for him to retrieve but he fired again at the birds. I couldn't figure why he was still shooting. He was only allowed by law to kill five birds. Unless he was a pretty rotten shot, he would have killed more than that by now.

I started walking along the shoreline towards Murray. I'm sure he couldn't see me. I wanted to see how many geese he'd got.

The snow was beginning to come down heavier now. Off to the west the sky had just opened up and let in a big swath of light on the scene. I came up behind a big rock by the shore and looked out at Murray amidst his dead birds. I counted eight dead geese. One was still flapping around, wounded. Murray ignored it. There looked to be a couple more dead birds floating in the open water not far away.

I ducked low as Murray turned, looked around, as if he sensed that someone might be watching. He picked up five birds, tied a rope around their necks and began to drag them back to his skidoo. The others he just left there, dead on the ice. Seemed to me like a pretty big waste.

I didn't want to move. He came so close that I could see the satisfaction on his face and then he waltzed off, dragging the birds to his skidoo.

After he packed his gun and tied down the birds, he revved up the skidoo and took off like a speed demon onto the ice, headed towards town. I was a little surprised that he wasn't sticking close to the shoreline. Instead, he was heading out towards the harbour, the most direct route home for him. Maybe the guy was in a really big hurry to go and brag about what he'd done.

As the sound of his skidoo began to fade, I went out to see if any of the geese were still alive. But by now they were all dead, even the one that had been flapping around. I picked up two birds and decided I would take them home to my mom, to fix for eating. But I wouldn't tell her who had killed them. Maybe Murray had overdone it a bit by killing so many, but I didn't really want to get the guy in trouble. It did bother me a little bit, though, because I'd heard Murray give a speech once and he had made a big deal out of calling himself an environmentalist.

As I came out of Back Cove onto the frozen ice along the main harbour I realized that the sound of the skidoo had vanished. I figured that Murray was long gone. I saw that the track of his machine had gone away from the bumpy ice near shore onto the smooth ice further out and I thought that this was not such a bright move. Even in the middle of the winter, East Harbour is a mix of salt and fresh water. There's a lot of open water out there and you don't want to trust going too far from shore no matter how solid the ice might appear.

The darkness and the snow were closing in around me. As I pulled my hood up and started to tie the draw string, I thought I heard something.

"Help me!" I heard coming from further out. I pulled my hood back down. "Help! Somebody, please!"

Chapter Two

A Hero's Secret

I looked at the skidoo track and read what it was telling me. The man had made a very bad decision. I looked along the shoreline, saw a fallen spruce branch. I grabbed for it and raced out towards the grey horizon, not sure in the half darkness where the ice would end.

I didn't weigh more than 140 pounds, I told myself. A skidoo with a big guy on it will go through long before I would. Suddenly, I saw the open water with chunks of ice floating in it. I saw the dead geese floating away. No sign of the skidoo; it was gone to the bottom. Then I saw Murray, hanging onto the edge of a shelf of ice, just scratching at it with his finger tips, trying to stay afloat as it kept breaking off and he slipped back into the dark, icy water.

"Just hang on!" I yelled to him and threw myself down flat on the ice. I reached the branch out in front of me towards the struggling man.

But I wasn't close enough. I watched as he lost his grip again and sank under.

Just then I heard the ice crack under me. I could even feel it start to bend under my weight. How long before I joined Murray? I wondered. What was I doing here anyway?

Still, I inched forward, keeping my legs spread wide, trying to distribute my weight, praying that the ice would hold. Murray's head was still below water when his groping hand found the branch and grabbed on.

Suddenly I found myself sliding forward. He was pulling me with him to a watery grave. *Let go,* a voice inside me screamed. Only I didn't let go. I dug in the toes of my boots. I even kicked hard enough to punch a hole right into the ice. That did it. I stopped sliding.

Murray was pulling himself up onto the ice as it still kept breaking under him. We were staring at each other, face to face. He was scared out of his skull. So was I. Neither of us spoke but I knew what he was asking me. *Don't let go, kid. Please don't let go.*

I could feel the ice going spongy again. Not a good sign. What exactly was my plan? I decided to just inch backwards, digging in my boot, punching it through the crust, the only way to get a grip. We began to move backwards, very, very slowly.

The cold was seeping through my clothes, right into my bones. I could feel the weight on my arm as I tried to drag Murray with me and I was starting to lose feeling in it, starting to lose my grip.

"Keep going," Murray said, his first words to me. The ice was starting to hold his weight. I watched as he tried to get up on his knees, though, and then fell forward, punching another hole into the water.

"Just stay flat," I told him.

I crawled backwards like that for a very long time. I didn't let go and Murray held on for dear life. It was like we were trapped in some crazy dance, flat out on this floor of ice, just staring at each other, not sure when it would be safe to let go of the branch and get up.

When we were close to shore, I knew the ice would hold. I let go of the branch and I tried to stand upright.

"I can't feel my toes," was the first thing Murray said to me as we both got up onto our feet.

We were both soaking wet. I could tell by the schizoid look on his face that he was still trying to recover his wits. "We gotta get moving," I told him. "Get that coat off. It's soaked and too heavy."

"I can't," he said. "My hands are numb." I unzipped the coat, threw it on the ice and gave the guy a gentle push to get him moving.

It was an ungodly hike back to town. We hugged the shoreline and I tried to make him jog so he wouldn't freeze up. I was cold, but I knew I'd make it. I could have left him and run for help but I decided it was the wrong thing to do. He might be frozen stiff by the time I returned.

Murray's house was on the edge of town, right on the water, one of the most beautiful old houses in East Harbour. We spilled in through the front door and fell down, letting the heat of the indoors flood over us.

Before Murray got himself thawed out in the shower, he told me to find some clothes to change into. I found a jogging suit that wasn't too baggy on me. He insisted I stick around for something to eat. He didn't want me to leave until we had a chance to talk.

He made us some coffee and that seemed to get him back in gear. "You're a bloody hero, Ryan. You're a goddamn hero. You saved my life. I'll never forget that."

Maybe that should have made me feel good, but I was still recovering from being so scared. It's funny how your mind works. I thought just then about the dead geese that were left lying out on the ice, geese that could have made a couple of good dinners. I wasn't about to go back for them. Then I thought about Murray killing more than he took home and I began to wonder.

"How come you shot so many geese and just left some of them on the ice?" I asked.

Murray suddenly looked baffled, surprised. It wasn't what he was expecting to hear from me. He said nothing as he got up from the table and went to a cabinet. He pulled out a bottle of whisky and poured some into his coffee, then offered me the bottle. I declined.

"Most hunters understand that many animals, especially in winter, suffer because of overpopulation. Sometimes it is the right thing... the environmentally sound thing... to thin a flock like that. That way they don't all starve to death. I couldn't use all the birds so I left the rest for other animals to scavenge for food."

"I guess I see your point," I said.

And then Tom Murray stood up and looked out the window into the swirling snow. "Would you mind keeping this whole incident — the hunting and my accident — would you mind keeping it between you and me?"

I guess the guy would have found the story a little too embarrassing. Adults are like that. And I figured just then that it might be okay to have a big timer like Tom Murray on your side. "Sure, Mr. Murray," I said. "I'll keep a lid on. It's just between you and me."

He pulled out his wallet and took out a fifty-dollar bill. He slid it across the table to me. I think it was maybe only the second time in my life I'd even seen a fifty. As I began to reach for it, I had this flashback to my old grandpop. Years ago, when he was still alive, he had given a tow to some crazies whose speed boat had gone dead. We were out fishing in the harbour. I was helping pull in cod and mackerel. One of the guys tried to give my grandfather money — a reward — but my grandpop had refused to take a cent. I don't think I ever understood why until right now. *You just do these things because you have to. It wouldn't be right to take money.* Those were the words of my grandpop.

"Forget it," I said. "You don't owe me anything." I went to the door.

"Wait," he said, as I picked up my wet clothes. "I haven't properly thanked you yet."

But I was already back out into the cold, snowy night and headed for home.

Chapter Three

Public Euphoria

The only person I told about saving Murray was Alana. Well, my mom found out, too, but I told her not to spread it around. I guess I felt okay about having the courage to save the man but I wasn't up to being made into a hero. I guess I did favour number two to Murray by not spreading the news and causing him embarrassment.

But someday, somebody will fish his skidoo out of the harbour and wonder just what *is* the story — where is the owner?

A week later, Alana was dragging me along to the public meeting about the new mill. It was snowing again, a fuzzy white softness coming down all around. I put my arm around her. "My mother's waitressing at the restaurant tonight," I said. "Why don't we just skip the meeting and go over to my house. I got *Wayne's World* on tape. We'd be all alone."

I knew she wouldn't go for it. I mean, she could be romantic and all that when the time was right ... but when the girl was serious, she could be very serious. "Maybe tomorrow night. Tonight we need to hear exactly what Alliance is up to. I don't trust them. Maybe I should ask your friend, Mr. Murray, about all the Micmac land they already ruined. Maybe I should ask him that."

Uh-oh. I heard that tone in her voice again. Very proud. Always willing to stand up to anyone. Sometimes it scared me a little. I stopped and made her turn toward me. We stood under a street light and the snow was falling down on her face. I looked into her dark eyes and I studied her face. She has a beautiful strength. I guess that's part of what scares me. I know she is smarter than me and in some ways stronger. If I wasn't head over heels in love with the girl, I think I'd rather be going out with someone who doesn't have such deep thoughts and a complicated mind.

"Maybe the whole project would go down the tubes if I had left Murray in the water," I said, just to see how she'd react.

"You couldn't do that," she snapped back at me. "You did the right thing. You did what you had to do."

And so we walked on. The community hall was packed. I'd never seen so many people out for a meeting before. Up front sat Tom Murray representing Alliance and, beside him, the MLA, Taylor DeLong, who was all smiles and politics and I knew that he'd help usher this project into existence. I knew because my father voted for him in the last provincial election. Heck, nearly everyone in town had voted for DeLong because of his promise to bring a pulp mill into East Harbour and "pump life" back into this town. My father had been practically promised a job here which meant he could stop driving all the way to Compton and living up there five days a week just so he could feed his family down here on the Shore. Having a mill here near town meant that I'd have my father living at home, not just a weekend dad.

"Okay, folks, settle down," DeLong said, staring through the smoke-filled air. "Let me start by saying just how good it feels to be here tonight and how much I appreciate all of you who supported me in the election and in my efforts to bring jobs back into this town."

Murray sat there looking confidently out at the crowd waiting his turn. In his businessman's outfit, there was no trace of the frightened man I had dragged out of the icy water. The fear in his eyes, the pleading — gone without a trace. I could tell that he had as good as erased it from his memory. Here was a guy who never had a second thought about his own abilities.

"Now, none of this is new to you," Taylor DeLong continued. "We've kept you informed every step along the way as to our progress. You know that Alliance has made a commitment and the province has made a commitment, as well, to Alliance and the people of East Harbour. So we're here tonight to say that we're ready to move on that promise. And, as you'll see, we're not just talking about an industry here. We're looking at a state-of-the-art, environmentally-sound operation that will be at the cutting edge in the field."

Cheers and applause went up in the room. The crowd was ecstatic and there was a party feeling in the air. I wanted to join in, but when I looked at Alana, she looked pretty unhappy. I wondered if it would have been better if we had both stayed away from this.

When DeLong introduced Tom Murray, people clapped loudly. A few even cheered.

It was a good thing I hadn't reported him to the game warden, even though I had thought about doing so a couple of times. Probably nothing would have come of it and besides, Mr. Murray liked me. Maybe if he still wanted to repay me, he'd make sure I got a good job at the mill a few years down the road.

"Thanks very much ladies and gentlemen. Like the Honourable Mr. DeLong, I too feel very good about being here tonight. Let me say it's been a long haul to do the planning on this project and to build the bridges necessary between my company and your community. But we're almost there and I think that we've been able to do it because of the good faith and support of all the people of East Harbour. And I think you all deserve a round of applause."

Everybody stood up and started clapping. Well, not everyone. I could see that a handful of fishermen — Reilly Driscoll, Bud Tillman and a couple of the old guys who used to fish with my grandfather — were sitting to one side. They didn't look too happy. And neither did Alana.

When things settled back down, Murray held up a picture of the proposed pulp mill. From the distance I was at, I couldn't really see many details, but the mill was surrounded by beautiful green forest and blue water and looked more like something out of a dream than real life. "Now, we'll have information packages available later this week for anyone who wants one but I wanted to show this little beauty here tonight. State-of-the-art all the way. And for those of you concerned about the environment, and hey, who isn't these days, I want to say right up front what's going on here. We will be cutting trees on land leased from the Crown and from private owners using only, and I stress, *only,* the latest and best forest-friendly techniques. And furthermore, no chlorine will be used to bleach the pulp. We plan to bring in post-consumer waste paper to an on-site de-inking plant so that our pulp ... which will be shipped out to places around the world ... will include a high percentage of recycled paper. And don't forget, we're talking about a significant number of jobs to start and possibly more down the road once we've established a position in the world market."

More applause. More cheers. Alana looked even more down at the mouth. I could read her mind. *It all sounds too easy, too good.*

Murray set another large poster up on a stand; this one was a map. He was pointing to a place on the map and, from where I stood, at the back of the room, I could see immediately what it was.

"We've kept a very low profile on this to avoid abuse by land speculators but now I can tell you that Alliance has purchased a 200-acre site here at Back Cove. We plan to do some work there to prepare the site, build the mill and dredge this section of the harbour so big ships can come in. And to ensure that absolutely nothing impure gets pumped into East Harbour, we're going to put a dyke across Back Cove here and use this natural resource as a settling and polishing pond. And for all this construction work, we expect to employ as many men and women of this town's labour force as we can."

Now a wave of confusion ran through me as people clapped. All of a sudden, instead of thinking about all the jobs in East Harbour, about how my father could come home and work close by, I started to feel angry about one thing: *Back Cove would never be the same again.*

Still, I sat there saying nothing as Murray opened the floor for questions. Everyone wanted to know things like exactly how to get on for the temporary work or what sort of permanent jobs would be opened up, what training the province would be willing to provide, and what improvements would be made to access roads to the forest in the interior.

Reilly Driscoll stood up. "What are the chances that this here pulp mill could kill off the fish? We've seen that sort of thing before, you know. We don't want to see the harbour choked up with sludge and we don't want to see *our* livelihood go down the tubes."

There were a few grumbles from the crowd, as if it was too much for *anyone* to question all the good news. But Tom Murray just smiled and nodded his head. He had it all under control. "I hear where you're coming from, Reilly. And I want you to know that not one fish will be harmed by this project. You and your kids and grandchildren will be able to fish in East Harbour for as long as you like."

It was an easy answer coming from a man who had nothing but confidence. Reilly didn't look convinced. "I hope you can be held accountable for those words," he said and sat back down. I watched the other fishermen and they didn't look too convinced either, but none of them stood up to speak.

Then, one after another, individuals lined up and asked questions at a microphone stationed in the centre of the hall. I had put my own worries about the cove on the back burner and I found myself getting caught up in the excitement again, so caught up that I hadn't even noticed that Alana was in line, waiting her turn at the microphone, until she was there ready to speak.

In a quiet powerful tone she addressed Murray: "I would like to know exactly where the pulp wood will come from, how it will be cut and how the forests will be managed."

A few voices of protest were rumbling — as if it was too much to allow for another question of caution in the midst of such euphoria.

Taylor DeLong interceded, feeling perhaps that he was the father figure here; he was the one whose job it was to protect the best interests of the people of the Eastern Shore. "I'd like to answer that, Tom, if I may. I want to say that the province will monitor to see that the wood harvested from the interior will be done in a manner that is both efficient and environmentally sound." He looked pleased with himself and his ambiguous answer.

There was a long line-up at the microphone with more people anxious to move on to other areas of discussion. Alana held her ground. "Does that include clear-cutting? Use of herbicides?"

Taylor looked over at Murray and wondered if he better get in on this question. Murray took the floor again. "Both have proven to be effective and safe in the management of a forest, if done properly." The words rolled easily off his tongue.

Alana spoke up again. "I don't believe you and I don't trust you. We do not want your mill," she said point blank. "We do not want what you will do to us." And she walked away from the microphone as men booed her and snarled nasty comments in her direction.

I was moving now and I caught up to her as she headed to the door. We didn't look at each other but went straight outside into the cold, clean night air. Once outside she put her arms around me and held on tight. I could tell she was trying not to cry.

"I was almost too scared to come out and say it," she told me. "Now I feel like I should have kept my mouth shut. Hold me, Ryan."

And I held her. We were alone outside in the parking lot. I held her and told her she did the right thing. "I'm proud of you for being able to stand up to all of them." I should have stopped right there but I heard myself keep on talking. "I don't think it's going to do any good, though. The town wants that plant. We need it."

Chapter Four

Indian Names

Two days later was Saturday. The snow was piled up everywhere but beginning to melt under a warm winter sun. It was one of those days you could feel the first tug of spring. Just when you get good and used to winter, everything changes. It was the way I felt about my life, too. We were in for big changes, all of us, and I didn't know if I was ready.

Alana is six months older than me. She had received her license over two months ago. On Saturdays, she'd get to borrow her mother's Honda and we'd go for a drive. She's a good, conscientious driver, not like a lot of the kids in my class who get behind the steering wheel and turn into maniacs. Alana is like the world's safest driver.

When her car pulled up I was out the door before she could get out. My mom was sleeping in after a long shift at the restaurant and my dad, who got in late after his usual Friday night drive home, wouldn't be up until around eleven. They both had it pretty tough. I felt bad I couldn't help out more. *Don't worry about it,* my old man said. *Just stay in school, buddy. Stay in school.*

"Where to today?" I asked Alana, settling into the passenger's seat and snapping the seatbelt. Once I forgot to put on the seatbelt and she gave me a long lecture.

"A surprise," she said.

"Let me guess. Musquodoboit? Porters Lake? Dartmouth?"

No answer.

"Your mom's gonna let you drive her car all the way to Halifax?"

"No."

"Where to then?" I could see we were heading east, not west.

"Nancy's Cellar," she answered.

"What?"

"Nancy's Cellar," she repeated. "Or at least the road to Nancy's Cellar. It's a name that used to be on a map. But they took it off, like a lot of the old names. They took off most of the old Micmac names too. My people had names for all the places but some were too hard to pronounce. Or maybe they didn't fit onto the road signs."

We made the turn up the old road towards Malay Falls and Lochaber Mines. It had been ages since I'd been up this way.

"We kept some."

"Some what?"

"Names," I said. I was trying to humour her because she was in one of her fragile, serious moods. "We kept Ecum Secum, Necum Teuch, Mushaboom."

"You think they sound funny."

"I like the way they sound," I said. "Stewiacke, Shubenacadie, Merigomish."

"All places where we lived." I know that *we* meant her Micmac ancestors, when she said it like that. But I also knew that when we got into these discussions, the differences between us became more noticeable.

21

She made me feel like "the white man." She made me feel like all the rotten things that happened to Native people were my fault, that "my people" did it to them.

"The snow is melting," I said. "Look, you can even see the ground."

She nodded. Just then we were at the end of the pavement. The car slammed into a serious pothole on the gravel road.

"They do front-end alignment in Nancy's Cellar?" I asked.

She slowed down a bit, negotiated each slush-filled pothole as it appeared before us. Nothing around but trees.

"Am I going to like it where we are going?" I asked.

"I don't know." Mystery all around. The girl was driving me crazy. I couldn't figure out what was going on in her head. Why do girls do that to guys, anyway?

In the middle of nowhere, she put on the brakes and got out of the car. I couldn't see anything unusual or special about this place. She began walking down a logging road and I followed. No trucks had been in here recently, but there were piles of logs hauled down from further in where they had been skidded out by the big machines.

"You don't see it, do you?"

I looked around. Spruce trees still coated with snow and ice. Some hardwood trees without leaves, brush.

"The trees they don't want are all dead," she said.

"Well, it's winter, remember? But they're not dead. What are you talking about? Spring happens. It all comes back to life."

"Wrong," she said. "This whole place has been sprayed with herbicides. Airplanes loaded with chemicals that kill hardwoods, berry bushes, weeds. It gets into the water. It gets everywhere. Kills everything but the spruce... because they take that for the pulp."

"So you're saying this is Murray's idea of good forestry?"

"Right. Listen."

I listened. "I don't hear anything."

"No birds. No signs of little animals. They are dead or have gone away. The spirit has been sucked out of this place."

We got back into the car and drove on. Alana gave me the silent treatment again. She was trying to prove a point. I wished she'd stop trying to teach me lessons and we could just go back to having a regular relationship. It was getting harder to hold back what I was thinking. *So what if you get rid of some alders and brush and a few weeds? What could that possibly hurt? It's just the way it is.* And it made sense to me to get rid of the unwanted trees so the spruce could grow better. That's only logical.

When we stopped again, it was a different sort of scene.

"Clearcutting," Alana said. "Look at that. It looks like somebody dropped a bomb on the place. How long ago was this done, do you think?"

"Two, maybe three years," I guessed.

We got out and Alana jumped over the stumps and the fallen logs to the middle of this clearcut patch that stretched out in all directions.

"Most people don't come back here to see this," Alana said. "The province owns the land and leases it for pulp. The quickest, easiest way is to cut down all the trees, leave what you don't want and haul the rest off to the mill in Compton."

"The mill where my father works," I added.

"Everyone has to work," she answered matter-of-factly.

"It'll grow back," I heard myself saying, echoing words my father had said to me years ago when I asked him about clearcutting.

"What they want to grow back, grows back. This all gets sprayed with herbicides too. No berry bushes, no hardwood trees. Only what they want. Even that will take years. We will be all grown up, maybe old by then."

I wasn't sure what she was getting at. I heard what she said but Alana over-reacts to environmental stuff. She is very idealistic and not always reasonable about the way some things have to be. "I don't think there's much we could do to change things," I said.

"Maybe not," she answered. "But someday they're going to have to stop doing this."

"You're probably right," I heard myself saying, climbing up onto the bridge of a fallen maple tree. I surveyed the junk yard of rotten wood. The snow was melting and uncovering what was left of the forest.

Alana was getting more angry now. "But they won't unless somebody makes them do it. They won't do it on their own. The wood for the new mill will leave more land looking like this. Destroyed. Dead." She was staring now across the acres of clearcut forest. "My father told me that this land belonged to us for many years."

"I know."

"No, you don't. We lost this land not so long ago. Back around when my father was born. My grandfather used to have a camp up here where he would come in the summer."

"What did he call this place?"

"You would laugh at the sound of the name. So I won't say it. But I'll tell you what it means in English."

"Okay, I 'll settle for the translation," I said, although I felt she was trying to build that wall up again between us.

"It was called the Place Full of Life."

And I didn't ask her anything more. We climbed back into the Honda for a slow, bumpy drive home, never having arrived at the mystrious place called Nancy's Cellar. I guess I still didn't really understand what she was trying to prove. She said that it was terrible what we were doing to the world. "All of us," she lectured. "We let it happen so we can have toilet paper and newspapers to read. And unless somebody takes you by the hand to see it for yourself, you don't care, you don't worry about all the Places Full of Life that once existed."

I could see her point but I didn't know why she had to take it so personally. It might have been something about her being Micmac. Or maybe it was just because she was a girl and girls let their emotions get in the way sometimes.

When we got to my place I persuaded her to come in and watch *Wayne's World*, and my mom and dad insisted that we ate supper with them. I prayed she wouldn't get started on the environment in front of them and my prayers were answered.

Chapter Five

Against the Entire Town

By Monday morning, Alliance's public relations campaign was in full swing and the town was buzzing with the "good news." A couple of the guys were razzing me about having a girlfriend who didn't know when to keep her mouth shut.

Chuck Engles cornered me by my home room. It was weird how he assumed that my opinions were the same as Alana's. "A couple of freaking tree huggers is all you are. I bet you both think we should all fade back into history, right. Leave the trees alone and live in little shacks, right? *Save the earth,* yeah? You two really go for that stuff ... but it's all just a line. It doesn't mean nothin'. You'll see. When the mill goes in and we all quit this dump of a school and start making good money, you're gonna miss out on it, buddy. Don't think they don't have your number."

"Engles," I said. "Did you hear me say *I* was against the plant? Alana's got a right to her opinions. Besides, she's not hurting anything. It's not like she can have any effect on the mill being built." And I think I realized then that I had just betrayed Alana, but I wasn't about to defend her in front of Engles. He and I go back a long way. He is a loudmouth but I understood where he was coming from.

Skip Tillman must have been listening in and Skip was always getting into some kind of row with Engles. "Chuckie," he said. "Think about how that mill could mess up the harbour. Man, did you ever think about anything but what's in it for you?"

And there was big, hulking, Davie Vaughan, leaning in on the conversation now, breathing down in a threatening way on Engles. Chuck was smart enough not to push these two, not unless he had a bunch of his own buddies around. He just shook his head and started to walk away. "Tree huggers and haddock heads," he said, "that's all you guys are." And it dawned on me just then that some kind of line had been drawn through the town with the fishermen on one side and everybody who wanted the new mill on the other. And then there was Alana, alone on nobody's side, and me, out on the side lines, confused.

That day we heard that we were going to have an assembly on ... you guessed it... "an informative presentation about the new mill." All the kids in school were going to get a rerun of the Murray and DeLong show. I thought, maybe I should take off for the day, but I remembered Alana and couldn't leave. I also realized she'd be the only one in the whole school who would stand up and ask questions. I didn't think Davie and Skip would say anything in front of everyone in the auditorium. Only Alana. And I'd have to at least be there to keep an eye on her and make sure things turned out okay.

For most of the presentations, the students were amazingly quiet and polite as DeLong blew hot gasses of political wisdom all over us and Tom Murray cracked a few jokes and spoke about a "bright new future" and "the dawning of a new era." They churned away for nearly an hour. Maybe some kids were glad to have an excuse to get out of a geometry test and catch a snooze in the back. Others were really lapping this up, dreaming of jobs and money. I wondered how many were already thinking like Engles: quit school, get a job, make good money and live happily ever after.

Then there was a bit of a ruckus down near the front and as soon as I could zero in, I saw it was Skip and Chuck picking up again on their argument from the hallway. I saw Chuck turn around and smack Skip in the side of the head but, quick as a flash, Mr. Clarke, the gym teacher, was on the scene of the crime and strong-armed both of them out of the auditorium. Davie was down there too with some of the other "haddock heads," as Chuck called them. I hoped Alana knew she wasn't alone in her opinions about the pulp mill after all.

I could see her across the room from me. She was sitting with Cathy, Beth and Doreen and my bet was that she had been trying to get them to see things her way. The hour was just about up. There were no microphones in the aisle this time, no opportunities for any of us to stand up and ask questions. Maybe that was just as well. Alana would stay out of it. She wouldn't rile up any of the other kids who might want to get back at her.

She turned just then and saw me. Her expression changed. She was reminding me of the road to Nancy's Cellar. Something would have to be done. I could tell she was about to get on her feet and shout out something. I thought that maybe if I got up and asked a question first, she'd stay out of it. If I did, I could keep her out of trouble. I'd be really calm and make it all very polite.

Before I gave it a second thought I was on my feet, interrupting Tom Murray. My hands were sweating and my head felt woozy as I spoke up as loudly as I could. "Pardon my interruption, Mr. Murray, but I have a question I'd like to ask."

Murray seemed only a trifle flustered as he paused and peered out into the auditorium. I waved so he could see me.

"Oh, it's you, Ryan. Sure, go ahead. We're just about out of time but, sure, let's have a question from the audience."

I saw Mrs. Deveau, the vice-principal, coming down the aisle in my direction and giving me a signal to keep quiet. I ignored her.

I wasn't really sure of what to say. "It's about the mill," I began with hesitation. "Actually it's about Back Cove," I continued, still trying to formulate something safe and sensible to ask.

Mr. Murray pounced on me with a nervous edge to his voice. "I don't think this is the time or place to get into *that?*"

I was puzzled for a moment, then it clicked. *My God. He thinks I'm going to ask him something about the geese and about pulling him out of the water.*

Suddenly I realized this guy was more than a little worried about the world knowing about his mishap on the ice. It gave me a feeling that I was now in control of the situation. I went ahead with more confidence. "Actually, there are several questions I wanted to ask about the *mill* and my guess is you can't answer them all now, but I would ask you to think about them." I was trying to sound clever and I knew I was no good at it. I nearly froze up and didn't know what to say next. Then the image of the clearcut land I'd seen on the weekend came into my head.

"Why do you use clearcutting and herbicide spraying on the forests? There must be better methods than that you could use. And why Back Cove? Why do you have to build your mill at one of the most beautiful coves in Nova Scotia?"

I could have continued with more questions. I wasn't really trying to give the guy a hard time. It's just that I was beginning to think about what might happen when the mill got built. Like Alana said, maybe there were some nasty side effects that should be considered. Most of all, I realised I didn't want to see Back Cove changed. I caught a glimpse of Alana out of the corner of my eye. She was smiling. I figured I had done the right thing, and I kept her from going off the deep end in front of the whole school. Hey, all I did was ask a few *reasonable* questions. Nobody could crucify me for that. It wasn't like I said we didn't want the mill, or, keep the jobs. I just did it for Alana, I told myself.

Murray backed away and gave the podium over to Taylor DeLong who had put his hands up in the air with a condescending expression on his face. "I can see your concerns, Mr. Cooper, and that's why I'm here to assure every last citizen of East Harbour, no matter how young or old, that my government will only give the final approval to this new mill if we find that it will not harm the environment in any way. That is a promise that I assure you we will keep."

I had an easy way out just then. I made my point. I should have sat back down. I was just about to do that, when I saw Alana was on her feet now. She shouted so everyone could hear. "I don't believe your promises. There have been other promises. Many of them. And they have not been kept."

A few catcalls went up from the back of the gym. I even think I heard somebody let go with an insult — the kind of Indian insult I'd heard only once or twice — directed at her.

But just then the bell rang. Taylor DeLong couldn't quite finish his sentence as the good old high school herding instinct took over. It was lunch time. No one wanted to hear any more from Alana or me or even from Taylor DeLong just then. All they wanted to do was feed their faces.

I saw the principal, Mr. Robertson, go up on stage and I knew he was apologizing to Murray and Delong. Mrs. Deveau, however, was on my case and she caught up with me as I found my way to Alana.

"Both of you in my office, pronto," she said.

Now, I had never really had any trouble with Deveau. She was okay if you stayed out of her way. When students got into trouble, they had to go visit Deveau and hear one of her obligatory lectures on "acceptable behaviour." A lot of the rough guys thought Deveau was a hard case and called her names — never to her face. I knew all those names and they were running through my head as Alana and I sat down in her office.

"I like your questions," she said right out, shocking us both. "You two have sharp, critical minds and are willing to speak up. I find that rather refreshing."

"You do?" I asked in disbelief.

"I do. But we still have a problem." She folded her hands together. "I want you to help me out by being more realistic. Be reasonable. You *can't* set yourself against an entire town ... the town you live in."

"Why not, Mrs. Deveau? If we're right, why can't we?" Alana asked.

"Well, hold on. I'm not sure you're right. If I was, I'd be behind you one hundred percent. I think it's good that you question these things — like you did at the meeting the other night. And maybe we should have had time for questions today. But you're going to have to be reasonable, or you might get hurt. And I can't allow that."

"We're not afraid of anybody," Alana said.

Deveau knew she was talking to a brick wall. "Look, I'll tell Mr. Robertson we had a good talk and you've decided to keep a low profile."

"We've only just started," Alana said, with me already wondering exactly *what* we'd started or where we were going.

Deveau rubbed her forehead. "If you are going to engage in a dialogue any further with anybody — Murray, DeLong or even the students who call you tree huggers, then you're going to have to do some research. Find out what you're up against and what *reasonable* things you can do to question the mill. You're going to have to know the facts. Maybe it'll change your mind. Or maybe you'll get them to consider some of the problems. Just be careful, please. That's all I ask. And no causing trouble at school or ... or we'll have to talk again."

Chapter Six

Two's Company

I really hadn't thought the whole thing through very clearly. I mean, I was standing up in public questioning this new pulp mill that would be run by Alliance Forestry Products, the same company that employed my father at their plant up north in Pictou County. I only did it because of Alana. I don't think it ever occurred to me that my old man would get flack for what I was doing.

Two nights after the school meeting, my father phoned from Compton.

"Ryan. How you doin' son?" he said.

"Are you all right?" I asked immediately. My old man never calls out of the blue in the middle of the week. He's a real penny pincher. Mom and I wouldn't expect a call unless he was hurt.

"I'm okay. But I was wondering about you."

"Me? I'm fine."

"Well, I'm not one to take much stock in gossip but I got a visit today from my supervisor here who says you and your girlfriend have been trying to stir things up at the meetings down there."

"You're kidding. It wasn't like that. All I did was ask a couple of questions when Mr. Murray was at the school." It seemed unbelievable that the news had reached my old man at work on the other side of Nova Scotia.

"You always did like to ask too many questions. Seems it got a few of the Alliance people worried. No big deal, I guess. Just sort of gave 'em a bad taste. Made 'em look bad. You know how them fellas in suits are always worried about appearances."

"Right. So they leaned on you to get me to shut up, is that it?"

"No. No. Heavens, boy. Nothing like that. You ask away with your questions. It's a free country. I wouldn't be calling you up long distance to tell you to keep your mouth shut. That wouldn't be the right thing for a father to do."

"What is it then, Dad? What am I supposed to do?"

"Well, Larsen here, one of the company men, he told me to invite you up here for a little tour. This here is an old plant, nothing like the new one, but he still thinks that if you come up and meet some of the people and see the operation, you might feel differently about the whole thing. He also said something about Murray wanting to do you a favour. Do you know what that's about?"

"I don't know. I guess. But it's not important. But sure, I'll come."

"Great. Larsen here says you have an in-service the day after tomorrow. Tell your mother to give you some money for the bus. Catch the bus into Halifax to the Acadian Lines and get a connection to Compton. The bus stops just about half a mile from the plant. If you can't make it back by night, you can stay over with me and miss a day of school. I'm sure that won't kill you."

I liked the idea of a chance to see my father. I really missed the guy and felt rotten that he had to work so far away, but there was something that felt funny about all this. "See you day after tomorrow, Dad."

As soon as I hung up, I knew that this was completely unlike my father. He was always so practical, so hard-nosed about spending money on things like phone calls and buses. Alana and I were just kids. What could we do to get in the way of a big corporation with the entire provincial government behind them? I guess Murray was bothered by us. And whether they had said it to my old man or not, I had the feeling that his future job at the new plant could be at stake. A lot of other men would want his position. Maybe they'd just happen to hire someone who didn't have a troublemaker for a son. What had Alana got me into? I wondered.

But right now I wanted to keep an open mind. Like Mrs. Deveau said, we needed to do research. And this would be part of it.

I phoned Alana and told her about the phone call.

"Interesting," was all she said. "Very interesting. Can I call you right back?"

"Sure."

She hung up and I sat there looking at the phone. The girl was always full of mystery. What was it with her?

Five minutes later she called back.

"Okay, Ryan. I can go with you. My dad says I can drive if you'll put your bus money into gas for the car."

"I guess that's okay," I mumbled. "But what I forget to tell you is that you weren't really invited. Just me."

Alana laughed. "That's fine. Don't worry about me. I'm just your little girlfriend tagging along out of curiosity."

"That'll be the day," I said. I knew Alana could never play that role.

We didn't talk about Alliance, Back Cove or the new pulp mill for the three hours it took to drive to Compton. Instead, we listened to some tapes of Midnight Oil, Guns 'n Roses, Tom Cochrane and the Hungry Lizards. Every once in a while we'd open the windows and sing along at the top of our lungs. Then Alana popped in a tape I didn't recognize. It was a woman singing and the chorus was the wildest, most out-of-this-world kind of thing I ever heard.

"What is that?" I asked.

"Buffy Sainte-Marie," she said, "a song called 'Sky-walker.' She was raised by a Micmac family."

I was blown away by the impact of the song.

When we stopped for coffee and donuts at Tim Horton's in Stellarton, we both had this kind of glow. I held Alana's hand and we acted goofy inside the coffee shop. I felt like we were completely free and independent and we had this beautiful thing together. Man, you should have seen the way that all those truck drivers in Tim Horton's were looking at us. But we didn't care.

As soon as the big smoke stack at Compton came into view, though, it was like everything changed. It was a kind of grey day with low-hung dark clouds and the pale grey plume of smoke coming out of the plant added to the eery effect. It felt threatening.

We pulled up to a chain-link entry gate.

"Made a wrong turn?" the security guy asked Alana.

I leaned over before she could answer. "I'm Ryan Cooper. My father works here and he invited me to come visit."

The security guy poked his head in the car, then looked at the clipboard he was holding. "Oh yeah. So you're Garrison Cooper's kid. Larsen said you'd probably be walking. Get lucky hitchhiking?" he asked, nodding at Alana.

Alana felt the sting of the insult with all its implications. She looked straight ahead. I saw her hands tighten around the wheel.

"She's with me. A friend." Then I added, "She drove me up from East Harbour." Oops. I realized that my explanation was a kind of slap in the face to Alana. I *had* succeeded in making it sound like she was just *tagging along.*

The guard waved us through the gates and we pulled to a stop in a visitor's parking spot.

"Did you see that look?" Alana asked me as she took the key out of the ignition.

"What look?"

"When he asked if we had made a wrong turn. He looked at me and I could read his thoughts. Indian. He probably thought I was someone from the Spruce Harbour Reserve. And just the way he looked at me told me everything about what his views are about Micmac."

In truth, I had read the signals but I wanted Alana to relax. "Nah. You're just being paranoid. The guy is a security guard. His job is to make people up tight."

We got out and walked towards the doors marked "Main Office."

A secretary led us to a waiting room with uncomfortable vinyl chairs and a pile of magazines with names like *Forest Industry Today*. A few minutes later, a door opened. Two men in suits walked in. One of them was Tom Murray. I wondered what the heck he was doing here.

Chapter Seven

Inside the Pulp Mill

Ryan," Murray said, "I'm really glad you could make it. I want you to meet Ed Larsen."

"Hi," I said. "Alana and I came up together."

I could tell immediately that they were both annoyed that I hadn't come alone. "Fine, fine," Ed Larsen said. "The more the merrier. Pleased to meet you, Alana."

We were given hard hats and led very briefly through the noisy part of the mill. Monster machines churned away mixing the pulp as Larsen tried to explain to us what was going on, shouting over the sounds of the machinery. There was no way you could call it a pretty scene but I guess I did find it fascinating. After a tour of the major workings of the plant, we were led toward another building and into a quiet, gleaming laboratory where people in white jackets were working. It looked like something out of a science-fiction movie. There was music playing in the background. "Wow," I heard myself saying, only to get nudged in the ribs by Alana's elbow.

"Impressive, isn't it?" asked Murray. "This is the heart of environmental control. Perhaps you'd like to just wander around on your own."

Alana and I walked away from Murray and Larsen and nobody seemed to mind us peering over their shoulders. There was an easy-going atmosphere in the lab.

Alana tapped a young woman on the shoulder and asked if she could explain some of what was going on here.

"It's pretty complicated stuff," she began. "Mostly we're testing levels of certain chemicals, the quality of the product, the safety of the effluent and that sort of thing."

"Thanks," Alana said. But as we walked on I knew she wasn't satisfied with the answer. "She could have been more specific. From that answer, they could all be just getting ready to bake a cake."

The whole morning had been peppered with little speeches from Larsen and Murray about how community-minded and environmentally-concerned Alliance was. It seemed that most of the time they ignored Alana and spoke to me. She said very little.

Later, I got to see where my father worked. He had a hard-hat on where he stood at his post monitoring a wall of gauges and dials and stuff that looked really complicated. The noise was very loud and he was wearing ear protectors like the men on the runways at the airport. When he saw us arrive he took them off and broke into a big smile. "Good to see you, son," he said. He was nearly yelling at the top of his lungs for us to hear. "Well, this is it. This is what your old man does for a living."

I could tell that he was really proud and glad I was finally getting to see him at his work.

"Your father has an important role here," Larsen said. "He's part of a very competent team and there's a lot of responsibility on his shoulders."

"It's just my job," my father said.

Mr. Murray cut in. "You know, we're pretty impressed with your son, too, Garrison. Ryan here has a good head on his shoulders and he's willing to stick his neck out when he has to. He's got guts. I think this kid will go far."

My father looked at me and nodded as if in agreement. "He's a good kid," he said, above the roar of machinery.

All the while Alana said nothing. My father didn't even seem to notice her until we were starting to walk away and he was putting his ear protectors back on. She was probably feeling ignored but I was flying high, feeling good about how these guys liked me. Just having a chance to see my old man like that, proud of his work, and getting a good plug from the guys in suits gave me a big charge.

We were taken to lunch in the executive cafeteria where my father joined us after a few minutes. He looked conspicuously out of place in his working clothes and I could tell he was nervous as we sat down to eat. He wanted to talk to me and I felt bad that we couldn't just then.

As he was going back to work he pulled me aside. "How's your mother?" he asked.

"She's working too much. Complains about all the time on her feet at the restaurant."

"Once I get moved down to the new plant, I won't have the extra living expense of being up here so she won't have to work any more." I knew just then that he said this intentionally for Murray and Larsen to hear.

"Gotta get back on my shift," he said.

I followed him to the door. "It's good to see you, Dad," I said, and softer, so no one else would here.

"You know, I really miss you not being around some-times."

There was a funny look in his eyes, like he was really looking at *me* for the first time in his life. "I know," he said. "I miss you, and your mother too. Sometimes that's just the way it is." And he was gone, back to work doing something with the monster ma-chines that mixed the pulp.

In the afternoon we were driven to a place where Alliance was planting young trees. It had the feel of a Christmas tree farm and I could see they weren't just cutting trees and spraying herbicides.

"This is the wave of the future," Larsen said. "This is where we *want* to go. Tree farming at its best. Replacing, renewing, regenerating forests." The R words rolled off his tongue.

"This isn't a forest," Alana said. "There is only one kind of tree — the kind you need for pulp. A forest needs to have many kinds of trees and other plants." I knew she had more she wanted to say but she stopped.

Larsen said nothing, just smiled politely and looked down at the ground.

When the day was over and we were being walked to the car, Tom Murray took me aside. "When you stood up in school the other day and asked those questions, I said to myself, *there is a sharp young man with a keen mind.* I was impressed. And it occurred to me then that in a few years, after you finish school and have a few years of university, that we'd undoubt-edly have a place for you. Probably right in East Harbour. You're exactly the sort of executive we'd be looking for — environmentally concerned, someone with an alert mind. And someone with the courage to, ah, well, do what you did for me when I got in difficulty. We *need* men like you."

It's a funny thing, but I still hadn't quite fallen for Murray's line. I mean, I felt good, I felt special. Well, none of those guys at school who talked about working at the plant had got a job offer, yet they were all crazy to get out of school. Here I was, confused and miles from home, practically being told I had a job for the rest of my life. I began to feel I owed Murray an apology.

As we got into the car and drove back out through the gate, past the smiling security guard, I realized how Alana had been ignored. No job offer had been made to her. To break the glacier that was starting to build up in the car, I asked Alana, "What do you think?"

"I think I want you to meet my Uncle George. I want you to see Spruce Harbour."

Chapter Eight

Uncle George — Medicine Man

Don't you think we should be getting home?" I suggested. "It's a long drive."

Alana turned left, taking us off the main road. "After today I think it's really important that you meet Uncle George first."

"Why?" I asked, a little annoyed. I really didn't feel like visiting Alana's relatives.

"They got to you, didn't they?"

"What are you talking about?"

"Murray and Larsen really did a number on you. You bought all that baloney."

"Not all of it," I said. "It's just that some of it made sense to me."

"Yeah, especially the part about needing someone like you as a 'future executive.' Don't think I didn't hear that."

Now Alana had turned her anger on me. She hurt my feelings although what she was saying had some truth to it. I liked the picture they painted and I wanted to believe that some day East Harbour would be a happy, thriving town. "Maybe it was just a pretty daydream," I finally admitted to cool things in the car.

Alana turned again, down a gravel road into a settlement of houses. She pulled into a driveway and stopped. When we got out a dog came running, barking at us. Alana called him by name and patted him on top of the head.

"Welcome to Spruce Harbour Indian Reserve," she told me.

The door to the house opened and out walked a very tall man in a flannel shirt and faded blue jeans. He had a braid of dark hair that hung down to the middle of his back. This was the famous Uncle George — the first Micmac medicine man I had ever met.

"Alana," he said and gave his niece a hug. He gave me a severe once-over but then held out his hand to shake. The guy had a grip like a sumo wrestler.

It was then that the wind shifted direction slightly and I received a powerful whiff of something that smelled pretty rotten. I winced and George said, "You think something smells pretty bad on an Indian reserve, huh?"

I shook my head no. The last thing I wanted to do was offend Alana's uncle.

But George laughed. "Look up. See the clouds move. Prevailing wind comes out of the west. Over there is the pulp plant. We're downwind from that place so we get to smell what becomes of those trees that get ground into pulp. You get used to it."

You couldn't see it in the air but it had a swamp-gas sulphury smell. And George was right. It did come from the pulp mill, yet the smell was stronger here than at the site itself where the smoke stack rose so high up into the sky that most of it blew away ... until it reached here.

"I was wondering if you could give us a ride in your boat," Alana asked him. "I want to show Ryan the harbour."

45

George studied her face for a minute. "The harbour is now cut off by a dam since the big fish kill in the Gulf. It's considered private property. No one is allowed to go there."

"I know that. But I thought you would take us anyway."

Now George studied me again. "Yeah. Sure. I got my boat on the trailer there. I always like a good excuse to put her in the water. Maybe stir up some fishing memories in our little harbour. The closest we can get to any fish these days."

We rode in George's truck back down the paved road and across the new dam that cut off the inland harbour from the Northumberland Strait. Someone had spray-painted on the road surface, "You are now in Micmac Territory." George drove us through a broken gate with a sign that said, "Absolutely No Trespassing." We stopped by the water. There were still some ice chunks around the shore and floating further out.

"It's beautiful," I said. I was expecting a harbour that looked like hell but this was entirely different.

"It's dead," Alana said.

I helped George get the boat in the water and he started the motor. When we were in the very middle of the harbour he cut the engine.

"This was once full of fish. All of us from the reserve fished here. It was our harbour. We have much love for it."

"I can understand why. It's very quiet, very sheltered."

"According to the government, we had no say in what became of this place. According to them it is no longer really a harbour. It's part of the pulp mill. It's *their* 'pond.' They pump the waste from the mill all the way over here so it won't pollute the waters near Compton. Here, the worst stuff settles before the water finds its way into the Strait."

"And in the process, it kills all the fish?" I asked.

"In the process, as you say, it kills everything. Even the pride of my people who love this place."

"That's not fair," I said. "If people all over Nova Scotia knew this was happening, they would have made the government step in to stop it."

George suddenly looked down into the water. I had to lean the other way for fear the boat was about to tip over as this big guy shifted his weight. "Funny, I almost thought I saw a fish. Wishful thinking I guess. My mind playing tricks. I used to catch thirty, forty pounds of fish here in an hour."

"Tell him about the government, Uncle George. Tell him how concerned they were."

George kept peering into the water, hoping for the fish to appear again. "Your provincial government came up with the plan to do this to Spruce Harbour. They made a deal with Alliance. Oh boy, everybody wanted that pulp mill and all those jobs so bad, they made a deal with Alliance. Said 'Build your plant. We'll take care of your water waste.' So the province did this to us. Pumped in the poison, killed the harbour and then put up a sign saying, 'No Trespassing.' What are they, worried we might come here and try to *steal* something?"

Chapter Nine

Worried Parents

On the way back to Uncle George's house, Alana explained about Alliance and their plans for East Harbour. George listened intently but said nothing. When she was through, George turned to me and said, "Last year, the government decided they had made a mistake. They apologized, gave $1000 to every family on the reserve to compensate us for our losses." He shrugged.

"That's nothing," I said. "You've all lost much more than that."

"We got used to losing things. Land being taken away. Nobody asked us first about a lot of things. Maybe I'm wrong, but I think it could be different now. We're all changing. You watch that stuff about Oka on TV?"

"Yeah," I said. "I did. I was thinking of Oka when I saw those words painted on the road back there."

"Young people just expressing themselves," was all George said.

"It wasn't just the harbour, Ryan. You smelled the air. People have to live with that all the time. A lot of kids have had breathing problems on the reserve. More than normal. Some had to go to hospital," said Alana.

"Some of our children have become very sick and a few babies have died," George added. "Nobody has been able to prove anything. Guess we're not quite smart enough yet. But we know we breathe a lot of bad air. And we know it's not good for the children. It makes them cough. What else it does, we don't know. And we don't eat as good maybe since we lost the fish."

It was dark by the time we got to George's house. If we left for home now, we wouldn't get there until late and I knew Alana had not had much practice driving at night since she got her license.

"You two wanna come in for something to eat? You're welcome to stay over the night and drive home tomorrow if you want."

"It's up to you, Ryan," Alana said. She wanted *me* to make the decision.

I didn't know what to say. My mom would go through the roof if I didn't get home, but I wasn't keen to drive all night. Maybe we should stay, I kept thinking, and it wasn't hard to see that an evening at Alana's uncle's house would be interesting.

Alana called home first and her father gave her a bit of a hard time until she put George on the phone. As soon as he got on, he started talking to his brother in Micmac. Aside from a few words that Alana used now and then, it was the first time I had really heard anyone speak Micmac at length. I was fascinated by the rush of sounds and the whole way George seemed to come to life when he spoke. And whatever he said, he seemed to iron things out so that Alana's father agreed that we should stay overnight.

By the time I phoned Mom, all I could tell her was that we were staying. I knew that putting George on the phone to speak Micmac to her wasn't going to quiet her worries. I had to phone her at the restaurant and I could hear the clatter of dishes and the hissing of the French fries as she was called to the phone in the kitchen.

"You're what?" she screamed at me when I told her I was staying the night.

"We didn't plan it. It just got late. We're staying at her uncle's. He's a very nice man." And then I added, "A medicine man."

There was silence on the other end, then, "Does your father know?"

"No."

"What would he say?"

"I don't know."

"Why don't you get Alana to drive you to stay with your father at the rooming house. Alana can stay there with her uncle."

I guess I hadn't been thinking of that angle. But I really didn't want to leave. "No, Mom. I'm going to stay here. I'll be home tomorrow. Now trust me."

I could hear someone yelling to my mother on the other end, something about customers not getting served. "I don't know what to do," my mom said, now sounding quite flustered.

"Everything is fine, Mom."

"But I don't know anything about those people."

It struck me just then that maybe my mom wasn't so much worried about me staying away for the night with Alana but that I was staying at the home of a Micmac family. "They are wonderful people. I'll be fine."

"You be careful," was all my mother could think to say. "We'll have a talk when you get home tomorrow."

"Sure. Goodnight."

"Be good, Ryan," she said and hung up.

While dinner was cooking, a woman showed up with a baby. I was standing there at the front door looking out at the water of the Northumberland Strait. "Where's George?" she asked me. The baby was wailing and I noticed it sounded like it was having a hard time breathing.

"Inside," I said and added, "Is your baby okay?"

She walked past me looking mean and sad. I followed her inside.

The woman spoke with George in Micmac. I didn't need to know the language to understand that she was very upset, that her baby was sick and that she had come to George for help. I watched as George sat down in a rocking chair with the child and sang softly to it. Even though the room was still full of other noisy kids and a loud television, George was able to calm the baby with his singing and soon the child fell asleep. When it did, he handed it back to its mother and brought her a small envelope of something. "This might help him sleep tonight. But take him to the doctor again tomorrow," George said.

The woman thanked George and left.

George was headed back to the kitchen as if nothing much had happened. "What was that about?" I asked him.

"That was about the pulp mill, Ryan. That little boy has very bad emphysema. He was not born with it. But now he can't breathe like he should and so he cries. I would cry too if I couldn't breathe. I gave her some herbs that might help quiet him but he will have to go in the hospital soon. He'll have to go into an oxygen tent and stay there for a long time. If he's lucky, he'll get better. But he'll have to grow up somewhere else where the air is better. He cannot grow up here."

All through dinner the sound of the little baby wheezing haunted me. The images of my day at the Compton pulp mill flashed through my head. My father standing at his post, smiling at me, proud of his job. The stainless, futuristic laboratory. The perfectly manicured tree farm. And then they were replaced by the still, dead waters of Spruce Harbour and the sputtering coughing and crying of a baby who could barely breathe.

After dinner, Alana and I played Monopoly on the living room floor with a couple of her cousins. Everybody played the game with so many jokes and so much laughing that it didn't seem to matter who was winning. It took me away from the scary thoughts that had been racing through my head, and I ignored the confusion that was building up inside and driving me crazy. When George switched on the hockey game, there was so much running commentary coming from everybody in the room that it was hard to even follow what was going on. After a while I got the hang of it and could join in. It was like a big comedy routine that we all took part in and I laughed so hard that tears ran down my face.

At nine-thirty there was a knock at the door. George got up to answer it. All at once I heard an angry voice. "Where is he?" I didn't even recognize my father's voice, but then it clicked.

"I want to speak to my son," he said, pushing past George and into the living room. I knew immediately that he'd been drinking. Now my father doesn't tend to overdo it often, but he does tend to get a little over-reactive when he hits the booze and I was fearing for the worst.

He looked like a bull ready to charge. "Ryan, who gave you permission to stay over with these people?"

"Well, I phoned Mom, and it seemed like the best thing to do under the circumstances," I said.

Someone had turned the sound off on the hockey game. A roomful of people were staring at my father. It was the most embarrassing moment of my life. I wished I could crawl under the couch or fly out the window.

"Well, you're not going to stay here. You're coming with me. You're my son and what I say goes." He wobbled a bit as he spoke, looking first at me and then at Uncle George.

"Was this your idea?" he snapped at George, who played it very low key.

"It was getting late and it is a long way to drive for two young people," George said matter of factly.

When he had walked in the room, my father was ready to go off like a stick of dynamite. He was probably expecting confrontation and I'd seen him go after a man with his fists once before for almost no reason when he was lit up.

"We should go," he said now, a bit more civilized. "Come on, Ryan. Sorry to disturb you all."

"I want to stay, Dad. I'm okay here, really."

The fire crept back into his eyes. I had said the wrong thing. I saw his fists clenching and unclenching.

"I got an idea," Uncle George said. "I'll get you a beer. You can sit and watch the game with us. You a hockey fan?"

Before my father seemed to realize it, George had put a beer in his hand and set him down in a big chair in front of the tube. Everyone got back to laughing and making funny comments about the game. Before the period ended, I even heard my father cracking a few jokes.

When the game was over and I was shown where I could sleep, I saw my father sit down with Uncle George, in the kitchen. I didn't know how much he had been drinking earlier and I was a little worried about him driving back to his rented room.

"Dad," I said. "You think you should be driving? You've had a bit to drink."

He looked down into his tea cup and swished it around. I think he was now feeling a little embarrassed.

"Sorry I stormed in like that," he said to George. "I guess I made a stupid move."

"You care about your son. You were worried," was all George said, then turning to me added, "It's okay, Ryan. We're gonna talk for a while, get to know each other. I'll drive your father back when he's ready."

"Goodnight son," my old man said, taking my hand and squeezing it once.

"Goodnight, Dad," I said and walked off, thinking that something very weird and very interesting had just happened tonight. Like Uncle George, the medicine man, had just worked some very powerful medicine because right then I actually felt closer to my father than I had in a long time. And I knew my father was feeling the same thing.

Chapter Ten

Just Say No!

Our trip to Compton made Alana more convinced than ever that Alliance and the province couldn't be trusted. What sounded like a great deal on the surface might turn out to be rotten for the town. I lay awake that night wrestling with some new worries that the trip had given me. Uncle George and the fate of Spruce Harbour were beginning to sit heavy on my mind. I remembered that putrid sulphury smell and I couldn't get the sound of the baby's crying and coughing out of my head. I was beginning to believe that Alliance's plans for East Harbour might just be pretty daydreams. How did we know that Back Cove wouldn't go the way of Spruce Harbour? How did we really know that the company and the government cared at all about the land, the water and the air?

Alana and I had been sitting in silence as the kilometres clicked by on the way home. She probably wasn't aware of what was racing through my head when I smacked my fist on the dashboard and said, "I understand now, Alana. I finally understand what you've been trying to tell me, to tell everybody."

At first she said nothing. Then, without taking her eyes off the road, she reached over and grabbed onto my hand and squeezed it.

"How much money do you have on you?" she asked. I was a little baffled. "My father left me another twenty-five bucks for gas. I think he was still feeling guilty about the scene last night."

"Would you consider chipping in for a worthy cause?" She gave me a devilish smile.

"I have a feeling I already have," I said, knowing I couldn't turn her down for whatever it was.

She pulled up in front of a print shop in Westville.

The guy who ran the shop didn't seem very busy and looked happy to see somebody walk through the door. "How many bumper stickers can you print up for sixty dollars?"

"A hundred," he said.

"Can you print them right away?"

"Sure. It'll take no time. Just tell me what you want on it."

"Hand me a marker and some paper."

Alana began to sketch something. It was a simple drawing but unmistakable — the outline image of the pulp mill in Compton with the smoke stack and the plume of smoke coming up out of it. She handed it to the guy. "Print in big letters right across the image the words, 'Just Say No.'"

"I think I heard that expression some place before," he said.

"It makes the point," said Alana. "What do you think?" she asked me.

"I think we are gonna make a lot of people angry."

"Maybe we can open some eyes," she said.

That was Friday. At school the following Monday, there was Alana's car parked in the lot with the sticker on the bumper. Kids were standing around talking about it. I was carrying about twenty stickers around with me in my notebook. Alana was standing by the front of the school asking some of the guys if they'd be willing to put stickers on their cars.

"How's it going?" I asked her, trying to pull her away from the goons who were not the least bit interested.

I walked her away from them and into the school.

"They think it's a joke," Alana said.

"Alana, all they can understand are the jobs, the money. I don't think you're going to change their minds." We were at her locker now. She set her books down on the hall floor.

"Ryan, I asked my father about the land around here. I asked him how come Indians own so little of it now. He told me that it was a combination of many things. Many Micmac died early on from the diseases brought by the settlers. Many were simply pushed off their land when the English gave it away out from under them. Much of what was left got whittled away when the province took control of the land, calling it crown land, supposedly to protect the forests. They even took over some places that my people considered sacred. Places like the forest around Back Cove. There were never enough of us around here to really fight back."

"But you can't do this alone," I said, pointing to the message on the bumper sticker. I could see where this was headed and I didn't want to see Alana get hurt. I couldn't let that happen.

"I'm not alone," she said, kissing me on the lips. "I have you on my side. And there will be others."

She caught me off guard, I guess, with the kiss. I didn't know what to say next. Other kids in the hall were watching. When Alana pulled herself away from me she took out another sticker, peeled the backing and slapped it down diagonally across her locker. "At least we have an audience," she said as the bell rang.

I lost track of Alana as I tried to play catch up in my classes. I had missed a quiz in English and a couple of homework assignments. When I was standing in line in the cafeteria, Chuck Engles "accidentally" knocked my books out of my hand and sent them flying. All of my "Just Say No" stickers were spread out there on the cafeteria floor for everyone to see.

"What's that supposed to mean?" Engles asked me as he stared down at the obvious message.

"We all have a right to our opinions," I said, trying to avoid being suckered into an argument.

"Cooper, I think you let your girlfriend brainwash you. I think she's the only one around here crazy enough to say no to the best thing that ever came this way. You know we're all getting a little tired of *her* opinions and the whole Indian guilt trip thing she tries to put on us."

I sucked in my breath and tried not to do anything dumb. There would have been a time when I might have just smashed the guy in the face with my fist but I wasn't going to be pulled into that trap. If I made the slightest move, there would be ten guys on me hammering me to the floor. "Thanks for the news," was all I said. "I'll try to keep that in mind."

As I was bending over to pick up my stuff, I saw Deveau walking towards us from the back of the cafeteria. She headed our way but walked past without saying a word. I had a feeling it was her way of letting me know that she was keeping an eye on things.

It wasn't until the end of the day that I caught up with Alana. I could tell by the look on her face that she had been taking some flack. "What is it?" I asked.

"Mr. Rutherford asked me what I was getting myself into," she said. "I tried to explain to him what happened to Spruce Harbour and all he said was that it was a shame, that someone had made a mistake, but it could never happen here."

"I have a feeling that people around here believe what they want to believe and nothing more."

We had just opened the door to the outside, about to step out into the spring air, when we were confronted with something we had never counted on. Over on the edge of the parking lot was Alana's parents' car. Somebody had taken a can of green spray paint and written "Tree Huggers Not Wanted" in big letters on the side of it.

"My mother's going to kill me," she said.

Chapter Eleven

Invasion Begun

While the bumper stickers were certainly not a big hit, Davie and Skip took a handful and I started seeing them on the trucks parked down by the wharf. A couple were slapped up on the sheds down there and I knew for sure that Alana and I were not the only ones who didn't trust Alliance and the province.

About a week later, CBC TV news had a story about the new mill. It turned out that the federal Department of the Environment had been working on their "assessment" of the project and had decided to give it thumbs up. I never really paid much attention to stuff like that on the news before. It always seemed pretty lame and very boring. Now I was beginning to wonder what it was all about. How exactly did they determine if this thing was going to be safe? How could anybody tell what might happen after five years or ten years? I was puzzled.

A news reporter shoved a microphone up to Taylor DeLong as he was walking out of the legislature in Halifax. "I think the people of the Eastern Shore have good cause to celebrate. This is another indicator that the new Alliance mill will be not only good for the economy of the province but also friendly to the environment. Of course, we are very thorough about this and, as many people are aware, we have our own provincial environmental assessment that has been underway for two years. We've hired the best consultants and we've had wonderful input from the public."

My mom walked in the room just then. "Ryan, I've never seen you so interested in the news before."

"Right, mom," I said, trying to ignore her and listen to the rest of what DeLong had to say.

"He sure looks happy," my mom said, pointing to the screen.

"Did you vote for him?" I asked.

"Yes, as a matter of fact, I did. Your father and I grew up with Taylor. He's not so bad for a politician. He always had high aspirations."

"I think he means well but he has blinders on."

"You're still worrying about what they'll do to Back Cove aren't you?"

"Yeah, Mom. I am. I don't like it." I switched off the set and was about to leave the house.

"I don't think you should be getting involved in this," she said. "You should be concentrating on your school work. Besides, it might not look good for your father, having a son who is starting to ask questions of the company he works for. I don't understand it. I don't understand what's come over you. It's Alana isn't it?"

Now, my mom had never had any real complaints about me and Alana except that she thought Alana seemed "so much older" than me. I guess that's true. Alana was always two steps ahead of me. "It's not just Alana," I answered. "It's Spruce Harbour." I had been holding back. I had told my mom that "nothing" had happened at Spruce Harbour. I was afraid she wouldn't understand what had happened to me there. But now I knew I had to tell her what I had seen.

"You're exaggerating," she said defensively when I was through.

"I wish I was," I said.

My mom sat in silence and stirred the tea in the cup in front of her. Then she looked out the window towards the harbour. "Reilly Driscoll and some of the fishermen were in the restaurant the other day. They were talking with Taylor DeLong. They were trying to convince him to go slow on the mill, that maybe it was wrong. You know Taylor. For him it was just like water off a duck's back. But a couple of the boys were getting a little angry. They don't want to see anything happen to the fish."

She paused, as if she was deciding whether to say anything more, and then she kept talking. "You were probably too young to remember but there had been an oil spill one summer — a tanker broke up down the shore and released thousands of gallons of heavy black oil. It killed off plenty of fish and wrecked lots of equipment. Nearly put your grandfather into bankruptcy. You never know what can go wrong. There's something pretty fragile about the sea."

Right then I think I was pretty proud of my mom because she had just shown me another side of herself, one she kept hidden most of the time. She acted like she wasn't interested in anything controversial, like she wasn't all that smart, but I could see that even if she hadn't been able to come right out and talk about it, she too had her doubts about the mill. She had been thinking about how it could change our lives, and not just for the better.

It seemed like a good time to leave so I hiked over to Alana's house. I found her father in their garage with a spray gun repainting the car. When he saw me, he popped off the face mask and smiled.

"I did a little body work. It needed repainting anyway. One of my hobbies." He seemed easy-going about it all, not like Alana's mother who had gone through the roof.

"Nice work," I said.

"The trick is not to put on too much paint at once or it runs. It's all a matter of patience."

"Alana around?"

"She's in the kitchen, reading."

"Thanks."

Inside, I found her reading a book called Bury My Heart at Wounded Knee.

"You weren't watching the news were you?" I asked.

"No, why?"

"Come on. Let's go for a hike."

We walked on down the harbour past Murray's house and found the trail through the woods that leads to Back Cove. I led her to an outcropping of rocks where we sat down in the sunlight and looked out over the little arm of East Harbour that would all-too-soon be changed forever.

"It's all going to be gone," I told her. "And it doesn't seem possible. I used to come here with my father when I was little. We'd sit here and he would tell me about the times he came here as a boy. Whenever I felt really messed-up I would hike out here and there was always something about being here, just being here, that fixed things. I never really understood it.

But I felt part of it all — the sky, the trees, the water. I never felt that way anywhere else."

"It's because this is a place of healing," Alana said. "I understand."

"I feel like someone is about to steal something from me. But I don't own this land and I can't do anything to stop it."

"How come you didn't say this to me before? How come you always act a little like the fight against the mill is all me... my idea and, apart from that one time, at school, that you are just going along to make me happy?"

"I've been a little confused. I'm not as sure about things as you are."

"But you're sure about this?" She waved her arm around at the view in front of us. This meant Back Cove and the way I felt about it.

"Yeah. I'm sure. And I didn't even know it until I heard DeLong giving his little speech on TV today. I kept thinking, has the guy ever changed out of his fancy suit and shiny shoes and put on some old clothes and come hiking here? Has he actually ever set foot on this place and thought about what would be lost?"

"Maybe he wouldn't feel what you do here. Maybe not everyone is capable."

"But you feel it too, don't you?"

Alana nodded yes. "I want to tell you something. It's not exactly a secret but it's something that my grandfather told me a long time ago. The Micmac families that are left on the Shore all know about this but we had promised not to tell white people about it."

"I don't understand. What?"

"This is a place of healing. It is a spiritual place. There was once a burial ground here. It's all grown over now. There's really nothing to see, but the spirit of the place is still alive."

"Why didn't you want other people to know?"

"White people always screw everything up. If everyone knew, they would come out here digging, looking for things. They would want to come here and root around. That would be bad for Back Cove."

"But now it won't matter. Now they'll change it forever. If this place has its own kind of spirit, what becomes of it? Does it die, does it go away?"

"I don't know," Alana said. "I guess once it's done, nothing will matter any more here."

We took a different route home, through the woods toward the highway. When we were halfway there, we came across four men in bright orange vests. Surveyors. They were tromping through the woods with their gear. We ducked low and skirted around them. I think we suddenly both felt as if an invasion had already begun.

When we got to the highway, their jacked-up four-by-four Jeep was parked on the shoulder. We both looked at it like it was some kind of evil monster. Alana was very upset. I was feeling pretty angry.

"Come on, let's go home," Alana said, trying to shake the bad mood we were in.

"No," I said, "I gotta do something. It won't make any difference, but I gotta do it anyway." And I bent over by the front wheel and popped the cap off the valve stem of the tire. Then I let all the air out until it was dead flat.

Alana was smiling now."Does that make you feel better?"

"A little bit," I answered.

"Let me try."

And by the time we walked off down the highway towards home, that Jeep had four seriously flat tires.

Chapter Twelve

A Done Deal

I thought that provincial environmental assessment would take a long time, but I was just a kid who didn't know much. Maybe I should have been watching the news or reading serious books all those years I was hiking around in the woods or goofing off in town. I just didn't think things were going to move so quickly.

"I want to show you something," Mrs. Deveau said to me in the hallway.

"What?" I asked. I was kind of freaked out that she had walked up to me like that out of nowhere. Had she been lying in wait for me? I was expecting more trouble. Did they figure out it was Alana and me who let the air out of the surveyors' tires?

"The province's report is complete. It's out."

She put a single sheet of paper in my hand.

"It's just the press release," she told me. "Murray just faxed it to the school. I made a copy. I thought you should read it. Come by and talk if you feel like it. Just don't start up any trouble in school over it, please." Her tone was sincere. She wasn't ordering me around; it was more like asking. Tough woman to figure out, Deveau was.

I read the first two paragraphs:

Nova Scotia's Environment Minister has released the environmental assessment of the proposed East Harbour pulp mill. Based on the findings of the study, the minister has decided to issue a permit to Alliance Industries to begin construction. The new mill is expected to be one of the most up-to-date and innovative in the world, including a de-inking facility that will recycle millions of tons of newsprint from around North America.

MLA for the Eastern Shore, Taylor DeLong, sees this project as, "the economic turn-around we've all been waiting for in this part of the province. With today's decision to approve the project, we expect that construction will go ahead almost immediately. The environmental review process has been in the works for almost two years. The people of East Harbour and all of the consultants involved have found that this is a sound proposal. There is no reason to delay."

I tried to read on but I had a hard time focusing my eyes. Once again I felt stupid. Maybe there had been some formal process going on for two years but why didn't *I* understand what was going on until recently? It was like I had been blind until Alana helped me see. In most ways, I guess, I had been like everybody else in this town. Now it sounded like the battle was over before it had even begun.

I skipped class and went straight to Deveau's office. "Have you read the report?" I asked her. "The actual full report, not just the press release?"

She shook her head, no. "I've phoned around. I can't find anyone who has. Apparently only 50 copies have been printed. But there is a copy down at the library. If you're interested you can just go in and read it. I think you and Alana should do just that."

"I want to read it," I said.

"So do I. But I'm not sure if it matters at this point. I think things are moving pretty fast."

Deveau had a worried look about her.

"You don't want this thing either do you?"

She threw up her hands. "One or two people with a few worries aren't going to be able to slow down this deal. It's just barrelling along. I'll be honest with you. I'm in a tough position to speak out with exactly what I feel. I admire you and Alana. But I still don't want to see you get hurt. And I think you're fighting a completely lost cause."

"Then why are you bothering to talk to me? Why did you show me that press release?"

"I wanted you to know you can talk to me about how you feel. It's part of my job, remember? I give kids heck when they get in trouble. And I try to head off trouble if I can."

Suddenly, I didn't feel such a big distance, that age distance, between Mrs. D and me. I saw her as someone trying to do the best she could but feeling trapped by it. She probably felt she couldn't even open her mouth at all those public meetings. She was fidgeting with her pencil now. I watched her try to balance it like a see-saw on her finger. "Alana and I, we don't think it's a lost cause," I said. Hearing myself say it, I knew that I had really changed. After Spruce Harbour, I couldn't just pretend any more that everything was going to be just fine.

Deveau put a finger in the air. She shifted again, back into her professional vice-principaled self. "Let's be realistic," she said to me. "When I was younger, I felt exactly the way you do. If I felt strongly enough about something, I thought I could change the world, right? But I had to learn to be realistic."

I wanted to say something really snarky just then about all this "realistic" garbage but I kept my trap shut.

"I had a talk with Tom Murray the other night. He invited my husband and me over to his house for dinner. I think I understand why the big push is on and why things are moving so fast. Their old plant up in Compton is losing money. It's going to be phased out. Soon. He says it's expensive to rebuild a new plant here instead of in the States or maybe even South America. Other governments have been pulling strings and making offers to get this plant. And if Alliance can't get moving on this thing here and now, Murray says the company will lose too much money. Productivity at the old plant is down — not competitive with the rest of the world. They have to close it, he says. If anything ... anything ... delays this plant by even a few months, Alliance might just pull up stakes and move to Brazil."

I heard all she was saying. And I understood. I just didn't like it. "What about Back Cove?" I asked. "What about clearcutting and herbicides?" I asked. "What are we gaining and what are we losing? It doesn't matter does it?"

Deveau sat motionless. "Don't over-react, that's all I ask."

"It's a done deal, isn't it?"

"Yeah," she admitted, sounding defeated.

I got up to leave. On the way, I pulled one of Alana's bumper stickers out of my notebook, peeled off the back and slapped it down hard across her door so that when it closed, the message would be staring her straight in the face.

Chapter Thirteen

Looking for Help

Alana was given detention for interrupting the "orderly discussion" in Mr. Rutherford's class again. I asked Rutherford if I could sit in detention with her and he said no, so I sat outside the school and waited.

When she came out of the building she looked depressed but when she saw me sitting on the wall, she smiled. "Waiting is one of the great skills," she said, taking my hand. "You knew I needed you."

"You know about the final approval for the mill?"

"It's not exactly a surprise," she said.

"I had a lecture today from Deveau about being realistic about it."

"Did it work?"

"No. I'm still out to lunch."

"How far out to lunch?"

"Far enough to ask you if you want to forget about this place and take off with me."

"You mean like run away?" Alana seemed genuinely shocked.

"I wouldn't call it that. I mean like just go some place else. Somewhere that people aren't so *realistic* and so mixed up?"

"Where's that?" Alana asked sarcastically.

"I don't know. We'll look until we find it." But I was just talking stupid talk because I was frustrated.

Alana laughed. "Nowhere to run, nowhere to hide. This is still the best place in the world. People here just don't know how much they've got."

"Until it's gone, right?"

"Yeah."

So stuck here in East Harbour and stuck with the inevitable future, Alana walked me home. As we neared my house, we both heard the noise of chainsaws in the distance. If Alana hadn't stopped dead in her tracks I might not have thought anything about it. It could have just been a couple of guys cutting firewood from the woods out by the highway.

"They're cutting trees for the access road to Back Cove," she said.

"How do you know?"

"I know," she said and I didn't question her further. I hadn't ever known anyone to cut wood out there by the highway. I remembered the Jeep and the surveyors and I knew she was right.

When Alana saw my father's car in the driveway she decided not to come in. It had been a long time since he had been home in the middle of the week. I should have known it was a bad omen.

I opened the door and there he was sitting in front of a beer at the kitchen table. My mother was home too. She stood over him, rubbing his neck.

My dad looked up when I came in and even before I could say hello, he said, "They fired me, Ryan. The bastards fired your old man."

"They can't do that," I said. "I was there. I heard Larsen say how good you are at your job. What about the union?" I knew my father belonged to a strong union that backed all their members when things went sour.

"I've already tried. The shop steward said he couldn't help."

"What reason did they give for firing you?" I demanded. Suddenly I felt mad at my father for letting it happen, for letting them, the bastards, walk all over him.

"After you came to visit —" he began.

"Oh my God," I interrupted. "You mean it was my fault?"

"No. Slow down, Ryan, boy. After I had talked with George there over in Spruce Harbour, I just wondered if maybe I *had* closed my eyes to a lot of things about the company I worked for. We were all like that. Didn't want to bite the hand that feeds. Heck, we just did our jobs, all of us. Never asked anything about the how or why of things. It's not like anybody ordered us to keep quiet. We just knew not to rock the boat. But after I heard George's story about Spruce Harbour and about the kids ... a few days later I asked buddy upstairs there if those stories could be true. I swear, that's all I did. 'You're gonna believe some old tales from an Indian?' Larsen asked me. And well, I knew what he was saying. I knew then and there that what George had told me was the truth. Only I couldn't come out and say it. Then it began to close in on me. If I said the wrong thing just then, Larsen would find some way to pull my job out from under me. I saw what had become of me — doing anything to hang onto my work all those years."

"So you told him to shove it?" I asked.

My mom gave me a dirty look like I had just said the wrong thing.

"No, Ryan. I didn't," my father answered, taking a sip of his beer. "I tried to weasel my way out of the tight spot I was in. I told him I was glad he set me straight. I said I was sorry to take up his time. And I went back to work.

"Here I am, a week later, with my walking papers. My supervisor said it had nothing to do with any talk with Larsen. Said it was safety infractions. They said they had been studying all the men and determined that I was a safety hazard to the whole lot of them. And there's not a shred of truth in it."

I watched as the frustration and anger boiled up in my father's eyes. He crushed the beer can in his hand and got ready to heave it across the room, but then, taking a deep breath, he looked at me and up and my mom and stopped himself. I had to look away just then because I'm sure my old man was about to cry. And I wasn't sure I could handle that.

"But it wasn't your fault, Ryan. Rest assured of that. You did okay."

My mother and father went to bed early and I stayed up to get my mind off of all the problems by watching a cable TV talk show hosted by some Nova Scotia writer who had once come to my English class to talk about writing. The guy was interviewing David Suzuki and talking about Suzuki's book called *Wisdom of The Elders,* something about aborigines in Australia and Haida on the West Coast and native people in the rain forests of Brazil. If my head wasn't so full of confusion, I might have found it really interesting, but the future was filled with questions now. I still knew that I was somehow responsible for what was about to happen to my family. There was no way I could get my old man's job back. Was Deveau right? Had I screwed things up by not being "realistic" enough? Had my curiosity and questioning of Alliance led to my father getting infected with doubt and losing his job?

On TV they talked on about foreign places, foreign people. Everything seemed so far away, so unrelated to my life here. I picked up the remote and got ready to flick the channel when a commercial came on — this really weird futuristic image of a man going up to something that looks like a pay phone and putting in money, and then cupping a mask over his face. The guy was paying to breathe air out of the machine. The message was loud and clear. There was a phone number flashed on the screen at the end and the word "Greenpeace."

I grabbed a pen and scribbled down the 800 number. Then I flicked off the TV and watched the screen blink down to dead. I thought of phoning Alana but looked at the clock on the VCR. Eleven o'clock. Too late. I didn't want to wake her family up.

But I wanted to talk. I wanted to talk to someone real bad. I looked at the Greenpeace phone number, started to dial, then hung up. Nobody would answer. It was after ten in Toronto. Even if they manned the switchboards at night, it would just be someone who wanted to take your money. And I wasn't about to consider donating any money to anybody. Our family was going to need every cent we had.

Greenpeace. Radicals. A bunch of over-the-hill hippies trying to save whales, climbing up smokestacks, hanging from the bridge in Halifax to keep out NATO ships. What else? Oh yeah, trying to save penguins in Antarctica. A bunch of crazies and show-offs. I never really liked their way of doing things too much. My father just said they were a bunch of rich kids who grew up and didn't know what else to do but cause trouble.

I turned down the sound on the TV as Suzuki and the host talked on and on. I dialled the number.

"Thanks for calling Greenpeace," a woman said on the other end.

"I'm not calling to donate any money," I said right off.

"That's okay. What can we do for you?"

"I don't know," I said. "I'm not sure why I called. Maybe I should just hang up. You're busy."

"You must have had a reason for calling," the woman on the other end said. She didn't sound annoyed which surprised me.

"I'm just curious," I said. "Are you like part of Greenpeace or just someone who answers the phones?"

"Both," she said.

"You ever do anything radical?"

"Hmmm. You mean like saving whales in zodiacs, that sort of thing?"

"Yeah."

"Well, I lay down in front of a bulldozer once at Temagami."

"Really? Why?"

She laughed. "I don't know what I was thinking. I got carried away. I didn't want them to cut down the trees."

It was funny how the word "trees" suddenly went off like a fire cracker in my head.

"I kind of have this thing for trees too," I said.

"Where are you calling from?" she asked

And before you knew it, I had told her the whole story. I couldn't believe I was pouring it out to this

76

stranger. When I stopped I almost expected her to ask for a donation. Maybe this was the way they suckered poor slobs like me into giving money. You call late at night, pour out your troubles and then feel better so you give these wackos a few bucks.

But she never asked about money. "I want to talk to some of our people about this. What would you think if we could get involved?"

I realized I was getting in way over my head here with some fanatic who had sat down in front of heavy machinery. My first reaction was to maybe just hang up. I hadn't told her my name yet.

But I didn't hang up. "What could you do?"

"Do some research. Start a small information campaign maybe, if you could get us some volunteers."

"There'd only be two of us. Me and my girlfriend."

"That's a good start."

"We could send someone to see you."

"No," I said immediately. I knew it was all wrong. I knew how this town would react to a bunch of outsiders, especially people from Greenpeace, coming in to stir things up. "No. Look, thanks anyway. It wouldn't work here. Thanks for listening, though."

"Sure. But if you change your mind. Call back. Ask for Mary."

"Thanks, Mary."

"I didn't catch your name."

"Ryan," I said. "Ryan Cooper."

Chapter Fourteen

Mrs. Deveau Plays by the Rules

Alana and I both got called out of home room to visit Mr. Robertson, the principal. Usually, if you're in trouble, you just have to deal with Mrs. Deveau. Anything requiring Raging Robertson meant really bad news.

"This bumper sticker thing has got to stop," he told us. "I've seen lots of kids like you two before. You don't really give a hoot about all the stuff you've been spouting off in classes. You just want to stir things up. Cause some trouble and have your brand of fun at other people's expense."

"That's not true," Alana snapped back.

Robertson wasn't about to hear anything we had to say. "I'm sorry, but I don't have time to hear your little song and dance. I know you insulted a guest to our school in front of the whole student body, I know you are being disruptive in class and I know you have no proper respect for authority. These things I will not tolerate in my school."

There was no point in saying anything. The guy was like a brick wall. No way to punch through all that denseness. Fortunately, the phone rang. It seemed important. Robertson wanted us out of his office, I guess, so he could talk. He muffled his hand over the phone and said, "I've discussed this with Mrs. Deveau. Go over to her office now. She'll spell out your terms."

As we walked down the hall to Mrs. D's office I asked Alana, "Terms? What the heck was that supposed to mean? Terms of punishment? For what exactly, I want to know? For opening up our mouths and asking a few questions?"

"It's like a conspiracy of silence," Alana said. "I expect we'll get a life sentence in solitary confinement now."

"I wouldn't let that happen," I told her, trying to break the mood that Robertson had put us in. "I couldn't live without you."

That made Alana smile. The last time I had seen her smile was when we let the air out of the tires of the Jeep.

I opened the door to Deveau's office. This place was getting all-too-familiar.

"Sit down," she said and nodding her head, added, "I know, I know. I'm supposed to dole out your punishment?"

"So what exactly are our *terms* of punishment?" I asked her point blank.

"I'm supposed to suspend you both and I'm going to do that."

Suspension meant that if we missed any work in classes, any tests, or anything, we couldn't make it up. If some teacher wanted to really get us, he could schedule something and there'd be nothing we could do.

"Look, I'll talk to all your teachers," she said. The lady must've been reading my mind. "Don't worry about that. And you know what Mr. Robertson wants. He wants you to cease and desist, as they say, all your campaign to stir things up against Alliance."

"What happened to freedom of speech?" Alana asked.

"Just hold on. *I* didn't say you should keep quiet. But what you have to do is come to me if anyone starts to give you a really hard time. Don't go head-on with anyone. Not teachers or students. You'll get crucified and Robertson will have his excuse to put on more pressure to keep you quiet."

"But what are we supposed to do, Mrs. D," I demanded, "sit on our hands?"

Deveau sat back in her chair. "You know, I went on a search around town to see who had read the provincial report. And guess what? Nobody had. Everybody had seen the press release or heard the news on TV or heard it first-hand from Murray. But the whole report is sitting down there in the library and, as far as I can tell, not one living soul in town has read it."

Now she had shifted gears. Again it seemed like she was on our side. "The 'terms' of your punishment are that I want you to do some research. Go to the library and read some articles on the next generation of pulp mills. Read up on the technology. But most of all, read the government report. It's not going to be easy, believe me. I took a look at it and it's pretty dense. But you're both all fired up about this. Read it. If you can each write a paper about what you found, I'll try to persuade Rutherford to accept them as extra credit. All I'm asking for is one day of real research during your day of suspension, which, by the way is tomorrow. What do you think?"

It was a little bit spooky. Here was the vice-principal taking sides with us. She was actually trying to set things up so we'd get credit for doing something we knew we had to do anyway. We *had* to get our hands on that report.

"It's a deal," Alana said and I seconded her words with a nod.

But there was something I wanted Mrs. Deveau to know just then: "Alliance fired my father. They fired him for asking questions."

"I'm not surprised," she admitted. "But I'm very sorry to hear it. It's not fair. I don't think anybody is playing by the rules and there's something fishy going on." Then she stared long and hard at Alana and the expression on her face changed. "Look, I really can't be getting involved like this. Just stick to the terms of the suspension. Nothing more, nothing less."

Alana and I walked out of there with a new respect for Mrs. Deveau but we were both baffled by something.

"I don't get it," I said. "We get dumped on because we're just kids. We're not supposed to know enough to have the right to question all the experts. But my old man asks one question and he gets canned. And Mrs. D, she's as worried about this mill as we are and I think she's afraid to open up and ask a few questions."

"Deveau is in line to be principal when Robertson retires, right?"

"Right."

"Well, if she doesn't play it by the rules, then she won't get promoted."

"But there don't seem to be any rules," I said.

"The rules are, you go along with whoever is in charge, whoever holds the power."

"People like Murray and DeLong?"

"Well, maybe not just them personally, but the people they work for."

"Those are the rules?"

"Yeah, I think so."

"But you and I make up our own rules, right?"

"Yeah, we've got our own game going. And they don't know what our rules are."

Neither did I but I didn't let on. Alana brushed her long dark hair out of her face and swept it over her shoulder. Whatever rules we were playing by, whatever game we were in, I knew we were a good team.

As we walked out of the office and out into the hall, I noticed that we were being watched. I looked up to see that it was Skip Tillman. The guy smiled and gave me a thumbs up and then just walked the other way. A lot of things were going on, but at least I now knew that we weren't completely alone .

Chapter Fifteen

Sludge Quotient Versus Pure Water

Alana was in a talkative mood the next day, as we walked downtown to the library. She had done a lot of thinking about what was going on. "We're going to have to study this report very closely," she told me. "Every word, every detail. Somewhere in there, we'll be able to see exactly what's going on. All that stuff Murray has shown the community — it's just a sales pitch."

"Why don't we go visit Taylor DeLong at his constituency office. Maybe we could get through to him."

"No. The province is putting up money for Alliance. They're in this together. I think DeLong would pretend he cared about what we have to say, but he'd slow us down. He's got a little formula that says, 'Bring in jobs and you bring in votes; bring in votes and you get re-elected.'"

"My parents voted for him," I admitted.

"So did mine," Alana said. "The lesser of two evils."

"I think you just gave me my first lesson in politics."

"I'll send you my bill for it."

It was truly one of those days when missing school was going to mean doing some hard work. As soon as we walked in the library, Margaret Brimer, a young woman who had recently got the job of librarian, zeroed in on us.

"How come you two aren't in school?" she asked.

"We were suspended," I answered and Alana proceeded to explain why.

"I can't believe they did that to you," she said sympathetically.

"Believe it," I said.

"I'm beginning to think that this town has gone a little crazy," she responded. "But I'm glad to see you decided to spend some time in the library. Can I help you with anything?"

"We'd like to do some research on pulp mills. You know, the whole technological process?"

"Sure," Margaret said, happy to be able to help. "I'll pull you a file I've been keeping on the subject — articles and statistics. All sorts of good reading stuff."

With the greatest of efficiency, Margaret found us the file and opened it on a table.

"But what we really want to do is read the provincial environmental assessment," Alana stated.

Now Margaret looked truly impressed. She walked to a display table in the centre of the room and picked up a large document. "Would you believe it's been sitting there since last week and only two people came in to look at it."

"Oh. Who?" I asked.

"Reilly Driscoll and Charlie somebody."

"Charlie Vaughan. They're both fishermen," I explained to the librarian.

I knew what this meant and so did Alana. Allies. The fishermen and their families were with us. We were going to have to talk to them.

Margaret continued. "They didn't stay too long though. They looked pretty frustrated. Then they stomped out of here angry as all get out."

"Weird," I said, as I picked up the report. Looking at it, though, I could see immediately what Driscoll and Vaughan would have been ticked off about. It was huge — intimidating. And it was filled with language that was nearly impossible to read.

"I guess we have our work cut out for us," Alana said.

"If there's anything I can help you out with, let me know," Margaret said and walked back to her desk. I watched her as she walked away and it occurred to me that maybe I had been wrong about librarians all my life. I had this idea that they were stuffy, creepy people who spent all their time telling kids not to talk; I had believed they were the ones who tried to keep kids from reading anything they thought was 'too adult.' But Margaret Brimer wasn't like that at all.

"It's over two hundred pages," Alana said, sounding intimidated.

She opened the binder to the first page and we began to read. I took out a notebook. The first couple of pages sounded a lot like the language that Murray had thrown around. Then it became very dense reading — it must have been very technical, written by a genius or a fool.

We ploughed on through page after page until well into the afternoon. Every now and then one of us would give up on the report and read through the articles Margaret had put together in her file on pulp mills. We took some notes. It was all very baffling. I was getting more and more confused by the details but I had this feeling that if we could just stay with it, just read every word in the files and in the report that eventually it would come together and make sense.

"What on earth is a 'sludge generation quotient' anyway?" I asked, finally frustrated and hopelessly lost in the maze of obscure language.

"I don't know," said Alana. "I've been reading for hours, but I don't know what I've read. And the library will be closing soon."

"We can't give up."

"No, we can't. But we need more time. We *have* to take this with us."

"I don't think we can do that. I don't think we'll be allowed to take this out of here."

"Ms. Brimer?" Alana said. "Would you mind if we took this with us?"

Margaret blinked as she looked up at us from her own work. "Sure," she said. "I don't see why not. In fact, keep it. I'll get another copy shipped out by courier from Halifax." I knew then for sure that this librarian was a real no-problem kind of person.

"Thanks," Alana said.

That night, Alana and I broke the report in half. She took the first half and I took the second. We sat up late into the night in my kitchen reading, jotting notes, looking up words in the dictionary. I called my father in to help explain some of the technical parts of the pulp-producing process. I even phoned Deveau a couple of times to ask for some help in figuring out some of the wording.

"Call me back when you've finished for the night," she said. "Tell me everything you learned. I don't care what time it is."

If it wasn't for the fact that it was all related to the changes at Back Cove, that it was all related to real life, I never could have ploughed through this stuff. But I knew that these words on paper, these stupid pages of numbers and technical mishmash were important. Somewhere hidden in this monstrosity of words and numbers was the real story.

Alana put her head down on the kitchen table to rest her eyes around eleven and she fell fast asleep. I stopped taking notes. I watched her, and wondered again how I had ever got involved with this mysterious, wonderful Micmac girl who had turned my life upside down. I touched her on the shoulder and gently woke her.

"Time for you to go home, sleepy head," I said.

"They'll be using herbicide on even larger tracts of land, won't they?" she asked me. She had not stopped thinking about the report. "More clearcutting too. Even the site will be stripped of all trees and levelled. It will look like the moon."

"It gets worse," I told her. "They're going to dredge the harbour. It will kill everything living on the bottom — but that is within acceptable parameters as the report says. Back Cove will be dammed off and become a settling pond. Remember the sludge quotient? Well, they plan to ship in old newsprint from all over the East Coast and they need a huge settling pond for the sludge. One sixth of the recycled paper pulp becomes useless sludge. It's full of toxic chemicals of all sorts, including lead and heavy metals. It will all get dumped into Back Cove where it will supposedly filter itself clean before going into the rest of the harbour. They've taken the chlorine out of the pulp process because the Europeans who will be buying the newsprint have demanded it. But they still haven't cleaned up their act. Not only are they going to wreck Back Cove but I don't believe that what's left of the water used will be pure. I think it's going to kill a lot of fish and God knows what else."

"So it's new, but it's not necessarily improved?"

"And here's the kicker. The mill will produce 50,000 tonnes a year but the really big improvement for Alliance to smile about is that once the plant is up and running, it will employ very few people. Everything is automated. Instead of 200 jobs, it sounds more like 30."

Alana looked stunned. "Let's trade," she said. So we traded halves of the report and continued on studying for what seemed like the most important final exam of our lives.

When Alana finally fell asleep at the kitchen table again and my eyes were too bleary to even focus, I called up Mrs. Deveau.

"It's two o'clock in the morning, Ryan," she said.

"You told me to call. That it didn't matter how late."

"Yes, I did," she said groggily. "Sorry. Go ahead. What did you find?"

"I found out that they are going to murder Back Cove, turn it into a sludge pit for old newspapers and that East Harbour is going to left with one hell of a mess, a big ugly pulp mill run by robots and only a handful of jobs."

Chapter Sixteen

Looking for Allies

There was a test in French the next morning and I
flunked it with flying colours. It was very hard to keep
my mind on school work, but Alana and I had both
agreed that, for now, there was no point in riling up
the other kids. Nobody would listen to us, anyway.
Besides, we had moved out of the arena of merely
trying to convince other teenagers that the mill was
wrong. We were in the big time now, and we were
looking for just the right place to throw the wrench
into the works.

At lunch we went to speak to Matthew Kern, the
editor of *The Shore Gazette,* the town's weekly paper.

Alana had the government report in her lap to read
out chapter and verse if she had to as I tried to explain
what we had found out.

"I've already been warned about you two," Kern said.
He wasn't even paying attention. "What do you think I
am, crazy? I can't print any of your wild ideas."

"They're not wild ideas," Alana insisted, holding up
the binder. "It's in here. Have you read it?"

He waved his hand in the air. "I'm a busy man. I
don't have time to read all that technical stuff. I have
a paper to run. Now give me a break. Write a letter
to the editor if you want. Maybe I'll print it. Keep it
short. But I still think you're wasting your time. That

mill is going to be the best thing that ever happened to this town."

End of audience.

"I think it's time we go looking for friends, instead of enemies," I told Alana as we walked down the street.

"What do you mean?" she asked.

"Let's go down to the wharf."

"Good thinking," Alana replied. "Maybe some of the fishermen are still interested in what's in the report."

We found Reilly Driscoll filleting some cod on the gutting table halfway out on the wharf. He saw us walking up to him but he didn't stop his work and he didn't look up.

"Hi Reilly, " I said. "Good catch?"

"Better than nothing," was all he said.

"We know you don't trust Alliance," Alana told him. "You probably know how we feel. I think we should work together on this."

But Reilly just kept cutting.

"We've read the report," I told him. "All of it. And we think it's much worse than we've all been told. Back Cove, the harbour, the forests they'll cut down for the trees. It's a nightmare. And there won't be that many jobs. Will you work with us?"

I knew that Reilly had always been the spokesman for the fishermen. They respected him. If we could get Reilly working with us, we'd have most of the men from the docks on side.

Maybe I had been fooling myself. When Reilly finally stopped filleting cod, he started to laugh. "You think we're going to throw in with a couple of kids? You must be nuts. The whole town would think we'd gone crazy, especially if we went along with you two."

"We need to stand up to this thing together," Alana asserted.

"Look, we think we already know that there's not a damn thing that will stop this mill. And we know that however it turns out it's not going to be good for the harbour. No matter what they say. If things go bad and we do lose fish, those fellows are going to have to compensate us. If that's the best we can do, we might have to live with it. But if we go along with a couple a kids, how much respect do you think the government or the company would have for us then? We might even lose a shot at compensation."

Reilly didn't have to tell us anything else. A couple of the other fishermen were staring at us now from their boats — Charlie Vaughan and Dick Lacey.

"Let's get back to school," I said to Alana. "I'm scheduled to flunk another test at one-thirty."

As we walked back towards town, Alana was still carrying the environmental report like it was a sacred book or something. "I'm going to visit Tom Murray," she said. "I'm gonna hit him between the eyes with some of this stuff."

"What's the point?" I asked, feeling defeated. I guess I had really thought that Kern would at least want to put a story in the newspaper.

"The point is that this is more important than school."

"Okay," I said. "I'm going too. I'll get an F on the Math test whether I show up or not."

Murray was sitting in his office, sipping a cup of coffee, feeling on top of the world. He greeted us like we were all the best of friends.

"Those are some pretty hard judgements," was all he said after hearing us out. "I'm impressed again,

Ryan, at your perseverance and headstrong interest in this thing. Sounds like you both really put some time in on that report. I just think you read a few too many of your own ideas into it."

"You're wrong, Mr. Murray," Alana said. "We seem to be the only people around willing to figure out what your mill will really do to this town and to the harbour."

Murray looked away from Alana and then at me. "I think you're over-reacting. Perhaps you've misinterpreted something."

"Go ahead," I said. "Tell us we're wrong about the sludge pond, about the spray and herbicides, and about the automation — the actual number of jobs at the new plant."

But Murray was cool as ice. "I doubt if you two are mature enough or technically astute enough to interpret that report. I'd say you did your homework but you did it all wrong. Now I think you two should be back in school, not down here jawing with me, cutting classes." Murray stood up, letting us know it was time to go. "And by the way, Ryan. I'm sorry about your father's job," he said as we got up and began to walk out of his office. "Real sorry," he repeated.

Alana fired him a look that would have melted steel. Once again, Murray had addressed himself only to me, as if Alana wasn't there at all, as if she didn't matter.

Outside, Alana turned to me and said, "It's an old Indian trick — invisibility." And I knew exactly what she meant.

We went back to a couple of classes to end the day at school and headed home separately. Alana kept the report and said she wanted to catch up on some sleep and then study it some more. When I got home I found my old man sitting in the kitchen with Taylor De-Long, of all people.

Taylor looked uncomfortable when I walked into the room.

"He's sure grown, Garrison," DeLong said to my father.

I wanted to say something nasty but my father quickly put me in the picture. "Ryan, guess what? Taylor here feels I was treated unfairly at Compton. He came to tell me that he'd look into it."

"That's great, Dad," I said without enthusiasm. I trusted Taylor DeLong just about as far as I could throw him.

"So while I'm looking into this problem at Compton, here's what I suggest," he said to my dad. "You know that road they're cutting in from the highway towards the Back Cove site? Go down and talk to the foreman. Tell him I sent you. I'll make sure you can get on there. You know, get some work going right away. And we'll see what else we can do beyond that."

My father shook Taylor's hand and thanked him with a little too much enthusiasm for my liking. By the time he walked Taylor to his car, I was beginning to get the picture. DeLong was worried that it might look bad if one of East Harbour's own men had just been canned at the Alliance Compton plant. He was trying to patch things up, make everything look hunky dory.

My dad was all smiles when he walked back in the door. "Taylor still thinks there's a good chance I can get on at the new plant when it opens."

But I was wondering about what my father had told me at breakfast. I couldn't understand why he was willing to go back to work for Alliance. "What happened to your plan to fish with Reilly Driscoll?"

My father shook his head. "I'd do it if I had to but fishing's a hard life. You saw what it did to your grandfather. And I did it for enough years to know that it's undependable. Long hours, low pay and these days there's hardly enough fish to keep an inshore fisherman in business."

I knew that what my old man was saying was true but, in my mind, fishing was at least honest work. It wasn't stripping the land of trees and pouring poisons in the water. I was a little ticked off that he was willing to go running back to Alliance, but I knew better than to argue with him.

Chapter Seventeen

What the Osprey Knows

Another week went by and the mill was that much closer to being built. Nothing could stop it. As well, my old man was going to be part of the work crew carving the new road out to Back Cove.

For Alana and me, a Saturday morning hike to Back Cove was becoming a ritual, now that the weather was warming up. It was the necessary reminder of what this fight was all about. The ice and snow were all gone now. The trees and plants had not come fully back to life yet but you could feel everything just about to break free from winter. The cove was alive with ducks and even a few loons. Red squirrels chattered in the trees.

Today, though, Alana could see that the trip here was making me even more depressed. Even on a weekend, the chainsaws were at work clearing the road heading towards the mill site. Soon it would be bulldozers and land movers and the end of this place.

"We're doing something wrong," I said.

"We're doing everything wrong," Alana suggested. "We're not getting anywhere. We've tried everything and nothing has worked."

"No," I told her. "We haven't tried everything. We've been trying to do this alone. There are people willing to help but we haven't let them."

Alana looked thoughtfully out at the water of the harbour shining in the sun. "Not just people," she said. "We haven't been willing to let the spirit of this place help us. We've been trying so hard but we haven't been paying attention."

She sounded so serious I almost convinced myself that I knew what she meant. It certainly seemed like I should know the "spirit of the place."

"If we go higher up over there on the hill, I'll show you the place that was once the burial ground of my people."

"There's nothing but rock up there. How could that be a burial ground?"

"The Micmac thought it was a good place to give the body back to the earth and the soul back to the sky."

"I'll take your word for it."

We hiked in from the water until we came to a steep place where there was a jumble of large granite boulders and a solid rock embankment that rose up about thirty feet.

"They'll take dynamite and blast this apart," I said. "They want it all to look like one big flat parking lot before they start building."

Alana said nothing but kept climbing. I followed. We'd both clambered around here before. Heck, I used to play games here with my buddies when I was a kid. And then I remembered a very curious thing. I had played cowboys and Indians out here with Robbie Robicheau.

And I had always been the Indian.

The sun was high in the blue, windless sky. Above us an osprey, maybe the first one of the season circled around. As it passed before the sun I felt a curious weight from the shadow of the bird and a chill went down my spine.

I looked at Alana. "You felt it too," she said.

"Felt what?" I asked, not wanting to own up to the quivering feeling I had in my gut.

"Close your eyes, Ryan," she said. "Tell me you don't feel it."

I closed my eyes just so as not to irritate her. And it was true. I could feel the weight of the shadow of the osprey again. I opened my eyes and he was right above us. I had seen him or felt his presence without even seeing him.

"That was pretty weird," I said. Suddenly I felt a little dizzy.

Alongside of us was a large, rounded, granite boulder. It sat alone on the rock shelf of this hill like it had been placed here on purpose. I knew enough geology to recognize that it had been left high and dry here by the retreating glacier. Nothing weird about that. But Alana was walking around the boulder, brushing off patches of yellow and grey lichen that covered it. The osprey circled again and I watched in fascination as the shadow of the bird made a perfect circle around the rock. Alana quickly followed the shadow around the rock, tracing its path with her hands.

And then the bird was gone. Alana began to scrape off the layers of lichen that covered the rock like old peeling paint. "What are you doing?" I asked

"I'm letting this place help us. It has been trying to but we haven't been smart enough to pay attention."

Alana kept brushing off the lichen in the circle around the rock until her fingers were scraped and bleeding.

"You've lost your marbles," I told her.

"No," she said. "Look."

All I saw was a groove that appeared in the rock all the way around. "Big deal. Erosion. Wind and water. Could have been a seam of something softer than granite there."

"No," said Alana. "Someone carved that into the stone. I think it means that this was the centre of something."

"The burial ground?" I asked, daylight beginning to break through into my foggy consciousness.

Alana looked around at the low walls of rock that surrounded the place on three sides. They were all grown over with ground juniper and scraggly stunted spruce. Between the plants, the lichen ruled. Alana walked to the nearest wall of rock and began to brush aside more lichen with a stick. This rock was not granite but some much smoother stone and it had been covered over with growth for years.

And then I saw it. It was an image of something — a bird, I think — carved into the rock. It was like something a kid would draw on paper but the more I looked, the more I realized how clear and perfect the image was, right down to the beak of the osprey.

Alana moved to the right as if plotting the path that this stone bird would fly in. She brushed aside some of the roots and vines. There was an unmistakable image of the sun. I ran to the rock further on and cleared away some of the debris on a shelf of rock and brushed the stone wall with my hand until I saw another image — a four-legged animal of some sort. I thought at first it was a deer but then I saw the antlers and recognized it as a moose.

I started to uncover some more of the rock wall but Alana stopped me.

"No. Don't. Let's fix this back to the way it looked. Others shouldn't see this."

"Why?" I asked. "This could be important. These could mean something. People should know." Already my head was reeling with excitement. We had found something. I wasn't quite sure what, but it seemed to send a glimmer of hope bursting through the back of my skull.

"White people call these petroglyphs but they don't know that they exist here at Back Cove. I had heard my grandfather talk about the rock drawings. He thought they might have been made a thousand years ago by our ancestors. They tell stories; they were put here in respect for the dead. They were not put here for the white settlers who would follow."

"But you can't just let them come and blow them sky high with dynamite. We have to do something."

"Yes, we do. But carefully. Remember, we haven't had much luck yet. We need to be careful. We need to do this right. You're always wondering why there are so few Micmac left around here."

I nodded.

"Once they took our land, there was little for my ancestors to do but move on. They had no power when it came to Englishman's laws and rules about ownership. When they left, so much tradition, so much knowledge, was lost about this place and about our past."

"But here is something we've found," I told her.

"I think maybe you're right but I want to talk to Uncle George before anyone else knows. Can you keep this quiet?"

I stared at the image of the moose and almost said no. Why waste time, I thought. We had to let people know about this so they could understand. Or would they understand? I thought about where the petroglyphs came from. I knew they weren't mine. I had no right to blabber my mouth about them. So even though it went against my instincts, I said, "Yes. You call the shots."

We returned to Alana's house where her father was at work repairing the kitchen stove. "You've been out to the cove?" he asked.

"Yes," Alana said. "The place of the round rock."

Alana's father stopped working, looked at me then back at Alana. "I think just maybe you broke a promise."

"Some promises are hard to keep," she said. "We found a drawing out there in the rock. I think there are more."

Her father stopped working. "It was once a sacred place," he said.

"It still is," Alana answered.

"You should call your uncle," her father said, waving a screwdriver in the air. "George should know about them. But he might be a little annoyed if he hears you've been letting others see them." I knew he meant me but there didn't seemed to be any real hostility in his voice.

"I'll wait outside," I said and went to sit on the back porch while Alana made her phone call. I liked Alana's dad just fine but I could see I had stumbled into something here and felt uncomfortable about being the centre of conflict between them.

About ten minutes later Alana came out.

"Uncle George was pretty excited to hear about the petroglyphs. He knew about the burial ground but didn't know there were drawings. He says there are other places like this around the province — Sackville, near Truro and on Cape Breton."

"What does he think we can do?"

"I asked him that. He says that, according to his understanding, Back Cove and all the land around it still rightfully belongs to the Micmac. There isn't even a treaty that he knows of where the land was turned over to the Crown. In other parts of the province there are treaties, but not here. Here, they just moved in and the Micmac were pushed away. George says that as far as he is concerned, Micmac people still own all the land at Back Cove."

"Then they can't possibly build the mill!" I screamed, jumping up and down on the porch.

Alana didn't look so enthusiastic. "No. George just said that like so many other things of our people, the land was just taken away and it would be impossible to get it back. He says it's not so different from Spruce Harbour. It didn't matter that the Native people protested. The government did what it wanted and nobody worried much about the Micmac. He said the same thing will happen here. He felt very bad that the petroglyphs would be destroyed. He said he would discuss the matter with the band council but he doesn't think there is anything they can do."

My heart sank and I waited for Alana to say more.

"Go home, Ryan," she said. "Please don't tell any-one about what we found. I'd prefer people didn't know. They've been hidden all these years. Maybe they should stay that way until the end."

As I walked home, I wondered why Alana was being so secretive. And I wondered how long I could keep the secret. It seemed incredible that I had never come across the rock drawings all those times I'd been to Back Cove. But then, I guess, I just didn't know how to see them. Maybe there were a lot of things that I hadn't seen up to this point.

Chapter Eighteen

Help from Greenpeace

Visits to Mrs. Deveau's office were becoming a regular thing. In our school, everybody knows when someone gets called in to visit the VP. It always means you are in trouble and Alana and I were sure getting a reputation for that. If you think about it, it was all pretty crazy. Other kids got into fights, drank beer in the washrooms or even broke into the equipment room at the gym to steal stuff, but they didn't seem to be getting nearly as much flack as Alana and me.

"I'm beginning to feel like a real criminal," I told Alana as we walked towards the office.

"You never felt this way before?" she asked. "You never felt like people were watching you all the time, expecting you to goof up and make mistakes?"

"No," I said. "I never did."

"That's interesting. I felt that way all my life."

And I think I just learned something again about Alana and about growing up as one of the few Micmac in East Harbour.

Deveau looked really uncomfortable. I was learning to read her like a book. I knew that she didn't want to be giving us a hard time. It was just her job. I wanted to let her know that I understood but, instead, Alana blurted out, "What now, Mrs. Deveau? What crime have we committed this time?"

"I think I made a mistake," she said, looking not at us but at the standard photograph of Queen Elizabeth on the wall. "I shouldn't have encouraged you to get further involved."

"All we did was research, remember?" Alana answered. "When has it been a crime to read in the public library?"

"I heard from Murray about your research. I guess I should be impressed. He thinks I should put some pressure on you to concentrate on your school work and ease up on extracurricular activities that might get in the way of your education. He thinks I can do something to tame your wild spirits." Deveau sounded exasperated.

"Mr. Robertson thinks I'm way too easy on you as well. You know what he's like. And now he has a hunch that I'm somehow part of this little conspiracy."

"And you think you just blew any chance you had at becoming principal when the old guy retires next year?" Alana asked.

"Well, I wouldn't say that but … ."

"So what are you going to do with us now? We haven't broken any new school rules. You can't punish us for what we do in town," I told her, trying to match the fire and the strength of Alana's point.

"Nothing really. I just want you to know that I wash my hands of anything you two have done or are about to do. I have my job here and I need to stick to that. I can't go bending the rules for anyone. Whatever you do, here or out there, you are on your own."

So she had just called us into her office to tell us she was wimping out. She had shown us a glimmer of her own views, her own doubts about the mill.

Now she was going to play it strictly by the book. She had sold out.

Alana was already three steps ahead of me though. "Mrs. Deveau, do you know what a petroglyph is?"

Deveau was caught off guard. "Of course. Native rock drawings."

"Back Cove is an ancient burial site of my people. There are petroglyphs there to prove it. Lots of them. They are very old, very beautiful. When they level the site for the mill, they will be destroyed."

Deveau looked stunned. "You're not lying are you," she said. It was a statement, not a question. "Why didn't you tell anyone before?"

"We didn't know," I answered and looking at Alana added, "Well, we didn't know for sure."

Deveau shook her head like it was all too much for her. She got up and walked over to the window. "This is incredible," she said. "If there are rock drawings there, then that's a valuable link to the past."

"Those rocks and the drawings belong to my ancestors," Alana reminded her. "They belong to the Micmac who are still alive. *That land* rightfully belongs to us. Not to the province, not to Alliance."

Deveau kept staring out the window. "Now what am I supposed to do?" she asked the clouds.

"You're supposed to help us," I answered. "Right now you are the only other person ... the only other white person other than me who knows about the rock drawings. You can either get in our way or you can do nothing or you can help us."

Deveau turned back to us. She had changed again completely. "Okay, you win. But what can I do? You know that they are ready to start clearcutting the mill site in three days. That road is complete enough to get equipment down there. Alliance has hired on every man in town who can run a chainsaw or drive a truck. They'll have the entire site cleared of trees in less than a week. Those boys want to move fast. They don't want anything to get in the way."

I guess I knew things were moving quickly. I just didn't know how fast.

"You need a lawyer," Deveau said. Then she corrected herself. *"We* need a lawyer. I can put up the money for the retainer," she said. "I can do that much and I don't care who knows."

Alana was sceptical. "But who could we hire? Who could we hire that we could trust? Not anyone from town here. They'd already be hoping to cash in on work for Alliance. And I don't even think we can trust anyone from Halifax."

Deveau nodded. "You're probably right there. A lot of lawyers in Halifax make a good part of their living in doing work for the province in some form or another. Many of them have tight political connections. It'd be a huge gamble to pick any of them."

Ever since seeing the petroglyphs I had been thinking about my phone call to Toronto, thinking about the phone number I had stuffed in my wallet. "I think there are some people in Toronto who might be able to help out," I said, pulling the phone number out. "Greenpeace. I talked to someone on the phone there. She seemed interested in helping out."

Deveau shook her head. "It's not a great idea. People around here would hate that. They'd see them as outside agitators. Radicals."

"So?" Alana asked defiantly. "If enough people around here don't care about ruining the forests and destroying Back Cove, then what does it matter where the help comes from. *I* say that all the white people who live here are outsiders, anyway. They all came from somewhere else. This wasn't their home. So what if we bring in other outsiders to help out?"

"Do you have a better idea, Mrs. Deveau?" I asked.

Deveau was silent. She looked over at the Queen again, like she was waiting for the her to give some better suggestion. But apparently the great woman had no bright ideas. Deveau pushed the phone across the desk to me. "Call," she said. "Tell them we need the best environmental lawyer their green brains can come up with."

Chapter Nineteen

Night Shadows

The first thing that surprised me about the lawyer Greenpeace sent down to us was that she was a woman. The second thing was that she was an Indian — an Ojibwa Indian from Ontario. Her name was Marie Smith and she arrived in a rented car late in the afternoon.

I could see the instant bond that developed between Alana and her. Alana explained the whole situation and Marie listened intently. Marie fired hard questions back and Alana answered them directly like she was taking some kind of very important oral exam.

Maybe I shouldn't say this, but I suddenly felt like I had been booted out of the picture. I tried to interject some of my own opinions but the two of them just kept going like I wasn't even there.

"It's pretty late in the game," Marie told Alana. "I don't know if I can do anything at this point. Why didn't you call us down earlier?"

Alana looked a little disheartened. "I guess I thought we could fight this thing on our own," she said, nodding at me.

Marie seemed to finally acknowledge my existence but she just shook her head. "The two of you up against all of them?"

"Well, I think most of the fishermen are on our side. They're worried that some fish might be killed off."

"So, have you been talking with them?" Marie asked.

"Yeah," I admitted, feeling a little foolish. "We talked with a guy who often acts as a spokesman for them. He said he didn't want to get involved with a couple of kids."

"You might just have to earn his respect," Marie chided us. "In these things, you need to work with anyone who shares your views."

"I think we are beginning to figure that out," Alana admitted.

I suddenly felt a little defensive and I guess my face showed it. I didn't want to hear anyone, even an Ojibwa Greenpeace lawyer, come here and try to make me feel like we'd been going about this in the wrong way.

"Relax, Ryan," she said. "I'm on your side, remember? I'll do what I can. But if I'm going to do any good on the legal side of things, I'll have to go to Halifax. I'll call you as soon as I can get something in motion. I'll try to let you know by tonight or tomorrow. Meanwhile, you two be careful. Anything could happen."

Then, as abruptly as Marie had arrived, she was off, out the door and back in her rented car, headed towards Halifax.

The next day passed and there was no word from Marie. I was convinced that it was too late; it was already all over. The gravel access road was now complete enough to get the machinery through. By the way, my father never did get temporary work on the road and, so far, he hadn't been called to work at the site. He was getting a little worried but he was convinced that DeLong would still come through with some kind of job for him to do. He wanted to work real bad.

Tomorrow was to be the worst day of my life. Cutting would start on the site itself.

"No call from Marie?" I asked Alana.

"None. I phoned the Greenpeace office in Toronto but only got an answering machine. I phoned Marie's hotel and left a message but she hasn't called back. I don't think she's getting anywhere."

"It's hopeless," I said. "We've been wasting our time."

But Alana didn't want to hear it. "Ryan, maybe it is hopeless. Maybe we have been wasting our time. But I don't think we should just give up."

There was a lot I could have said just then ... too much probably that would have revealed a big difference in the way Alana and I saw the world. I figured it *was* hopeless and we were wasting our time. Why waste any more? Just get out of the way and let things happen. But for Alana it wasn't over. There was a point to made here, a message to be spoken no matter how many deaf ears it fell upon. "So what do we do next?" I asked, keeping my thoughts to myself.

"We make signs; we go to the site first thing in the morning and make sure that anyone who comes out there to watch or to work knows that we believe this mill is wrong."

"I'm with you," I said, trying to muster as much enthusiasm as my unconvinced self could muster. "And we call up Bud Tillman, Reilly Driscoll and every fisherman we can get in touch with along the harbour. We invite them to come protest. It's up to

110

them after that. If they want to laugh at us, so what? Maybe Driscoll will see how serious we are."

"But can we trust them?" Alana asked. "What if they tip off Murray?"

"I think we have to take the chance."

"Agreed," Alana conceded.

It was the middle of the night, maybe twelve-thirty and I was involved in a nightmare. I was running through a deep, dark forest and the trees kept falling all around me. I could hear them crashing but I couldn't see anything and I knew that any second a tree was going to come down on my head and it would be all over. I just kept running and running, wanting to scream but nothing would come out.

And then something woke me. I was in a cold sweat. Somebody was banging on the glass of my window. At first I wondered if a storm had come up in the night. It must have been the branch from the apple tree banging away there. But I opened one eye and then the other. I jumped up out of bed. There was a face at my window.

"Ryan," Alana said. "We've got to go there. We have to go there now."

I was trying to pull my head together. There was Alana looking at me through the window. I suddenly realized I was standing there in the moonlight in my underwear. I grabbed my jeans from a chair, but when I tried to put them on, I tripped and fell on the floor.

When I finally wrestled my way into my pants, I opened the window. I expected Alana would begin to laugh hysterically at me but she was dead serious.

"Ryan, we have to go there now," she repeated. "We can't wait for morning."

"Why?" I asked. "What's going on?"

"You'll see," she said. "Do you know the woods well enough to get us through there at night? It's the shortest way."

"Maybe," I said. "I'll give it a try." I pulled on a shirt some socks and some shoes, threw on a sweater and climbed out the window to join Alana.

As we headed along the shore of the harbour, Alana stayed very close to me but she wouldn't tell me why we were going there now. The moonlight shivered on the waters of the harbour in a mystical silver glow. It was a cold night but beautiful. We could see our breath hang in the air as we hiked along and I heard the piercing shriek of a great horned owl searching for prey. I knew the shortcut through the forest to Back Cove by heart. It wasn't really a trail at all but I had walked it a thousand times and always thought I could get there with my eyes closed. Now was my chance. As we moved out of the moonlight and beneath the shadows of the big spruce trees, my dream came back to me. Were we about to be crushed by toppling trees? Alana was holding onto my hand now and I could tell by the pressure that she was feeling a little bit spooked too.

"There's nothing to worry about," I said. "I used to come out here at night all the time." But I was lying.

Once we got so far in that I couldn't see the moonlight reflecting on the harbour, I really wasn't sure of my bearings. I tried to relax and go on instinct. The trick was trying to stay in a straight line. It really was like a dream after a while, not a nightmare exactly, but it seemed so unreal. Just when I was ready to confess that I thought we were hopelessly lost, Alana said, "There," and pointed to a glimmer of light that I could barely make out through the trees.

"What is it?" I asked.

"You'll see."

As we approached I could see it was a fire of some sort. My imagination leaped to all kinds of crazy conclusions. I thought of the petroglyphs and of the burial grounds. I thought of the spirits that Alana had spoken about.

"This is crazy, " I said. "This is totally nuts." I was sure we were about to meet up with the ghosts of her ancestors or maybe something even weirder than that.

As we emerged from the forest, Alana leading the way now, I could see the roaring blaze of a campfire and twenty, maybe thirty dark figures huddled around it. We had arrived at the access road, at the very end of it where, tomorrow in daylight, the clearcutting of the site would begin.

But I wasn't worrying about bulldozers and chainsaws right now as I stared at the flickering fire and heard the shadowy figures speaking in a language that I could not understand. The fire, the night, the people — everything seemed like a surrealistic dream, real enough, but still a dream.

Chapter Twenty

Clearcut Confrontation

As we came closer, I saw someone get up — a large broad-shouldered figure. He came our way and I shuddered as he reached out and touched me on the shoulder. Then, speaking to Alana not me, said, "You brought your friend to us again, I see."

To me he said, "Come, sit down." And I didn't take another breath until I was seated with these apparitions and realized that they were human and as real as me. It was Uncle George who had spoken. "Good to see you, Ryan Cooper," Alana's father said to me. And I saw her mother sitting beside him.

The rest I didn't recognize but Alana quickly explained. "They came down from Spruce Harbour to help us. It was a surprise to me too."

A woman poured me a cup of tea and put a blanket around Alana and me. Aside from the crackling and popping of the fire, there was only silence. No one wanted to explain to me exactly what was going on. No one needed to. We were alone, together, the thirty of us, with this place, this forest on the edge of Back Cove that might be gone in a matter of days. I shuddered again, not from the cold, but from the weight, the gravity of the situation. At first it scared me. I was in over my head. But then I listened as a woman on the other side of the fire began to softly sing something in Micmac. The sound of her voice drowned out my fears and as I held Alana close to me there in the dark night, I felt a strange, powerful sense of urgency sweep over me. The forest was still there; the cove still untouched. There was time yet for something to change.

In the morning, not long after sun up, the fire was extinguished and people mulled about making jokes, chatting like it was no big deal. We were all waiting for something to happen, waiting for the world to find us and for the confrontation.

When the first cars and trucks arrived at around eight o'clock we had formed a blockade across the roadway. There were no signs, no protestors' pickets, just us — some sitting in lawn chairs, some sitting on the ground, others just standing and waiting. No one looked anxious or upset. Nobody on our side of the line that is, anyway.

As men got out of their trucks to gawk at us, I recognized fathers of some kids from school. Some were laughing. A couple shouted insults at us. And then a car drove up the middle of the road and I knew who would be the first to tell us to get out.

Tom Murray squinted up his face from behind the windshield. As he shoved open the door and jumped out of his car, I could see the rage in his face. The old women sitting in lawn chairs beside me clucked their tongues, like they were about to chide a small boy for losing his temper.

Murray stormed towards us and when he approached the line, looked around at the faces. No one on our side stepped forward to speak or assert any leadership. Even Uncle George and Alana's father were hovering off to the side.

"What the hell is this?" Murray finally screeched, directing the question at me.

"We don't want your mill," I said. "We tried to show you it was all wrong for here. We can't let you destroy Back Cove." I kept it simple.

"You can't destroy sacred land," Alana added.

"That's bunkum and you know it," Murray said.

Now Uncle George stepped forward. "To you, it may be nonsense, but to us, it is not. You tell your men that they can't cut down these trees because you do not own this land. This is our land."

I thought Murray was going to blow a gasket. I watched as his face went red. He looked square at me with an expression that said he wanted to kill me.

But he couldn't. He couldn't get away with it in front of an audience. Instead, he blustered back to his car. I watched as he pulled the microphone of his two-way radio outside and called the Mounties. This was the inevitable move. Now that I was in this thing up to my ear lobes, I wondered if George or Alana or anyone had any sort of strategy. What would happen next? Would we all get arrested and dragged off? Or would the workers, anxious for the work and in need of the money, go for us first and beat the living daylights out of us?

Instead of chaos, however, I was surrounded by a sea of Micmac calm. One older woman in a lawn chair opened up a large cloth bag, took out some yarn and began to knit.

I heard the scratch and roar of Murray's speaker phone. The Mounties had heard his message loud and

116

clear and were on their way. I knew in a flash that half the town would know also about this immediately. There was a radio scanner in the hardware store and in the restaurant and in many people's houses. We were a community with little excitement except when disaster struck or a crime was committed. Word would get around quickly and pretty soon, we'd be staring down all of East Harbour as well as the Mounties. Perhaps even more importantly, the fishermen would hear. Bud and Reilly had sounded doubtful on the phone. They still didn't want to get involved with us. They didn't commit themselves to anything. I wondered how they'd react when they heard Murray's angry voice on their radios.

Another woman started knitting and a couple of the men had begun to reminisce about the old days, the good old days, fishing on Spruce Harbour. The workmen stood around their trucks and cars, fidgeting. A couple started up their chainsaws and revved them, as if in a kind of threat. Townspeople began to arrive by the carload now. The news was out.

Bud, Reilly and five other fishermen drove up together. I saw Davie and Skip sitting in the back of one of the pick-up trucks.

"Well, we're here," Bud said to me as he surveyed the crowd of Micmac with suspicion. "You really think this'll do any good?"

"Thanks for coming," Alana said, instead of answering his question.

"Oh, well, can't hurt to try," Reilly conceded and walked over to join the people from Spruce Harbour.

"What the heck," Bud added. "Come on boys."

And we found that we had just increased our numbers by five good fishermen and a couple of other kids from school.

The RCMP were pretty slow in making it to the scene. Taylor DeLong arrived and stood beside Murray, trying to look calm and respectable, his most notable skill. And then my parents showed up. With them was Mrs. Deveau. All three of them walked towards us, towards me.

"Ryan," my father said, "son, this will never work. Give it up now before you get into big trouble."

"I can't, Dad. We're all in this together. It's something I have to do."

My mother looked frantic. I was afraid she would cry. "Listen to your father, Ryan. Now, before somebody gets hurt. There's *nothing* that will do any good. Alana, please. You too. I don't want to see anyone get hurt."

"It's okay," George said to me and then looked at my father. "Ryan doesn't have to be in this if he doesn't want to. We would understand. He's already helped and we appreciate that."

And as George locked eyes with my old man, I watched my father's face go through a range of changes. I knew that he admired George. I knew that he was scared for me. I could see the confusion in his face now. He didn't know what to say next.

From behind them, I saw Murray was really restless. The RCMP still hadn't arrived. Murray was telling the foreman and the other men to just walk past us and get to work. "They have no right to do this," he was shouting. "Just ignore them. You want the work. Get to it."

So we were all just standing there when ten guys with chainsaws started walking our way. Now, the noise of a chainsaw is never a pretty sound and I could tell by the look on some of the guys' faces that they expected us to just back away and let them through. It's hard to say exactly what they intended. My Micmac friends seemed pretty cool. The fishermen looked nervous but we all just stood our ground and even the ladies knitting in their lawn chairs didn't move. The tension was building, though, as the roar of the chainsaws grew louder. Some of the workmen had already begun to simply walk around us. A few of the Spruce Harbour people were trying to get in their way, but none of them threatened the workmen in any way. Suddenly Mrs. Deveau and my parents were coming towards us as well.

"You men just back off for now," said Mrs. Deveau to the men. "Wait for the Mounties to get here. Wait for the authorities to sort it out." I guess she still thought this was school and she was trying to play her role of authority.

But Robbie Robicheau's father and one other guy kept coming right at us, not around us. The blades of the saws were aimed at the ground but the noise was deafening. I saw the look on Robicheau's face. He hated us for what we were doing. He would like nothing better than to see us chicken out and back off so that he could get past and start cutting down trees.

I was the one right in Robicheau's path. If anyone was going to have to get out of the way, it was me. Alana was holding on tight to my arm and her father was tugging at me now to move out of the way. He didn't want to see anybody get hurt.

Then my mom panicked and screamed at my old man, "Do something, Garrison. Stop them!"

I think my father was really afraid I was about to get hurt and when he heard my mom scream, he reacted. He felt he had to do something. So I watched as he stepped forward, saying, "That's far enough, Jim. Just back off until we sort this out."

But Jim Robicheau kept walking. My old man freaked and grabbed Robicheau by the arm. He spun the guy around as he yelled at him and the chainsaw came flailing right at my old man.

"No!" I screamed at the top of my lungs, as the spinning teeth of the chain blade cut into my father's leg. He cried out and fell to the ground. Robicheau couldn't seem to understand what had happened but I wasn't about to take any chances. I kicked the saw out of his hand and it went buzzing and rattling onto the ground.

Chapter Twenty-one

A Question of Ownership

My father was lying on the gravel with his face twisted up in pain as my mother rushed to him. Jim Robicheau looked shocked and afraid as he backed away. I knelt by my father and looked at the wound in his lower leg. The cut was deep and there was a lot of blood but my father said, "It's okay. It didn't hit the bone." Leave it to my old man to try to play it macho at a time like this.

"We have to get him to a hospital," Mrs. Deveau said.

George leaned over and looked at the bleeding. He tore off his shirt and, placing it over the wound, he began to apply pressure.

Then things went crazy. Other men were starting to move forward. All they knew was that trouble had started. One man ran toward George and pushed him away from my father.

I screamed at the guy but he lunged at me and pushed me down. Then all at once, all of the men were pushing through the line of Micmac. I saw Alana ready to punch somebody and I quickly ran to her and pulled her aside before she could get in a shot. Some of the Micmac men and women had tried to stop the workers and fights were breaking out. Reilly and Bud came to the rescue of these strangers from Spruce

Harbour and found themselves throwing fists at guys they'd probably known all their lives.

Just then the RCMP car arrived and a lone cop jumped out. He was a young guy and I could tell he was freaked out by what he saw happening. I watched as he hopped back in and got on the radio. No doubt he realized he was in need of some backup. Then he jumped out of the car with a bull horn. "All of you, just back away," he said. "I repeat, everyone just back away."

But his words had little effect. Finally, he took the rifle out of the front of the car and shot up into the air. Everyone stopped and there was quiet as the young Mountie, looking nervous, walked forward, his rifle held upright in front of him.

As he neared us, Tom Murray and Taylor DeLong approached him. I couldn't hear what was being said but I knew it was their side of the story.

Together, they came up to where my father was lying on the ground. George had returned to him and was still pressing down on the wound. It had stopped bleeding but there was one heck of a mess of blood on his clothes and on the ground. "I'm okay," my dad said. "It was an accident."

Maybe my dad was cool, but I sure wasn't. It was Murray who had brought on all this trouble and it was time to say what needed to be said. I walked right up to his face and spoke loud enough for everyone to hear. "I saved your freakin' life, you bastard, and then you have the company fire my father. You want to destroy Back Cove and now this!"

My fists were clenched in rage. I could have done just about anything next. I wasn't thinking clearly. The Mountie walked up to me and just said, "Move back away from this man, son. Just move back." I took a deep breath and backed-off. Everyone was looking at Murray now. Everyone was wondering what I was talking about and sooner or later, everyone would know the true story of that day last winter.

Both sides had pulled back now. The workers were behind the cop, the Micmac and the fishermen in front of him. It was registering in his brain that he was staring at a crowd made up mostly of Indians. I watched the guy's throat muscles go tight as he was trying to size up the situation, probably figuring that he had just stepped into another Oka incident.

"Who's your leader?" he finally said. "I want some-one to tell me what you're doing here."

No one said a word. Alana looked at her uncle but he nodded to her. She was to speak for us all.

"This is rightfully Micmac land," she said, her voice shaking a little. "Behind us there is a sacred burial ground. No one has a right to come here, destroy the forest and build a mill that will chew up more forests and create poisons for the harbour."

The Mountie didn't know what to do next. I think he was praying for his backup to arrive. Taylor De-Long leaned over and began to say something to the cop but Murray had lost his ability to keep cool. He walked up to Alana, his face a contortion of anger, and screamed straight in her face, "You have no right to do this. You *can't* do this!" Then he turned to me and shouted, "It's all your fault, Ryan!"

Taylor DeLong, realizing that Murray could only make things worse, walked over to him and pulled him back. He tried to quiet him down but not before Murray shouted to the Mountie, "I want you to arrest them for trespassing. I want you to arrest all of them," he said sweeping his arm in our direction.

But Alana, her parents, the people of Spruce Harbour and their new allies had re-formed into a line across the road. A couple of lawn chairs were being picked up and the old women were being settled back into place as if nothing had happened.

Behind the Mountie, another line had formed — angry men, some of them holding tire irons or pieces of pipe and wood. I watched Mrs. Deveau, who was now left in between, in the no-man's zone. I guess she finally had to choose sides and make a stand. She walked towards us and stood beside Alana and me.

And then something very weird happened. George and my mother helped my father up on his good leg and, together, they hobbled over to join us.

"We're not leaving," George said.

Murray pointed a shaking finger at us and screamed at the Mountie. "Arrest them all, dammit. Do your job!"

I heard the sirens of two more police cruisers approaching. The cars stopped and four Mounties got out of their cars. But behind them was someone else. It was Marie, our Greenpeace lawyer. She walked straight up to the young cop and Tom Murray, wielding a piece of paper.

"This is a court injunction," she said, loud enough for everyone to hear. "A judge has ruled that this land may rightfully still belong to the Micmac people. Nothing can happen here until the courts determine its ownership. As it stands, only the Micmac and their friends have a right to be here."

Taylor DeLong snatched the paper out of her hand and looked long and hard at it. "I'm afraid she's right," he said to Murray and then, turning to all of the people from East Harbour who had come to watch the chaos, he said, "Everybody, please go home now. Nothing else is going to happen here today."

Now Murray turned his rage on DeLong. With the whole town watching, he screamed at him. "You can't just walk away, DeLong! Alliance is losing money every single hour this project is delayed."

But Taylor just threw his hands up in the air in resignation and kept on walking.

Murray turned back and fixed his eyes on the lawyer. "I'll be more than glad to see you in court, lady," he said, then turning toward Alana and me added, "I hope I see all of you in court and I'll see that you end up in jail where you belong."

Chapter Twenty-two

Back Cove's Secrets

When the first day of summer finally arrived at Back Cove, it looked pretty much the same as it has on the first day of summer for hundreds of years. There were long shoots of new green growth on the spruce trees. A pair of ravens stood guard on the branches of an old maple tree and the moss underfoot was soft and lush, green as green could be.

My feelings for Alana had grown deeper now. Rather than feeling intimidated by her strength and convictions, I felt like I had learned from them. This is not the sort of thing a guy like me can usually own up to but I can say it now. Before, I had been weaker than Alana but she had given me a chance to be her equal.

I knew we were in love but it was different from all the other kids at school. I'd watch guys goof around with their girlfriends — teasing them, making out in the hallways, or sneaking off in their cars after school. But we were never like that. Our relationship was different. I don't think anybody, even my parents or Alana's parents, fully understood us.

But we understood each other.

Lawyers were still arguing in courts as to whether the Micmac had any rights to the land. Marie expected it could go on for years. Greenpeace had set up a fund and people from all over Canada were donating money to keep the court battle going. People across the country suddenly cared what happened to Back Cove. So I guess some things had changed. And I guess I knew now that two people, two teenage kids, could make a difference. They could save something worth saving.

For a while, we all took a lot of flack. Alana and I got the stone-cold stares or took verbal abuse from kids at school. My mother was noticing she got less in tips at the restaurant. No work came through for my old man so he ended up buying a chainsaw and cutting firewood to sell. He took a course on selective cutting and he was managing his woodlot in an environmentally responsible way.

So, for all of us, things were more difficult — but better.

Alliance hadn't pulled out yet. They had been pressuring the province but ever since the court injunction, the whole issue had become complicated and "political," only now the politics seem to be working more *for* us than *against* us. It's amazing what a little national publicity can do.

One afternoon Alana and I were sitting by the petroglyphs at Back Cove as the raven's caw echoed across the harbour. We were sitting, letting the place speak to us again. We hadn't told anyone but Mrs. Deveau about the rock drawings. It will come up in court if necessary but only if it is necessary. And we hadn't uncovered more of them, still hidden by lichen and moss. There is this feeling that sacred things should not be exploited. Maybe that's what this place was always saying to us.

The silence we were sharing was broken by the sound of footsteps. Someone else was climbing the gentle slope of rocks. Someone was coming our way. Alana and I strategically placed ourselves with our backs to the exposed rock drawings.

When we looked up, we were shocked to see Tom Murray. He had found our secret spot.

He was surprised to see us but said nothing and shook his head.

"What are you doing here?" Alana blurted out.

I expected a confrontation. I expected him to be angry, maybe even violent. I was prepared to punch the guy's lights out if I had to.

But he was just looking down at the ground. Then he sat down on a rock. "Trespassing, I guess," he said, "by your way of looking at things."

"Yes," said Alana.

"But it was a beautiful day. I wanted to come here. I wanted to try to understand what all the fuss has been about." His words sounded honest, not mocking.

"This is what it's all about," I said to him. "The trees, the sky, the water down there."

"It's a beautiful place," he admitted.

"Then why try to destroy it?" I ask.

"Ryan, I don't think we ever wanted to *destroy* anything. It's a matter of trade-offs. Compromises. Prices we all have to pay to make a living."

"There's a good chance you'll lose," I reminded him. "You might not get to build your mill here."

He shrugged. "Then we'll have to go someplace else, I guess. I've stopped worrying about it. It's out of my hands now. I was doing my job, and I hope I still have a job after this is all over."

I wasn't about to feel sorry for the guy.

"You know," he said. "Deep down maybe I kind of admire you two kids. Willing to risk your necks, willing to stand up for what you believe in and not back down when the competition gets tough. And brains to boot. If we had people like you working for Alliance, we'd be ahead of the pack. We'd be the most profitable company in the industry."

Alana looked at him like he was crazy. I thought she was going to laugh in his face.

"No, I'm serious. Think about it." Murray picked up a stone and threw it high into the air, out over the cove. "Ah well," he said, getting up to go. "I won't ruin your picnic any further. I better be going before someone has me arrested for traipsing on property that doesn't belong to me."

As he got up to go, Alana had the final word. "It's not property, Mr. Murray. The land doesn't really *belong* to anyone. No one can really *own* the land or the water or the air. We can use it but we shouldn't destroy it."

Murray didn't answer. He walked on down the slope. I was thinking that maybe he'd heard it all before. Maybe he'd just go back home and go back to his job and think the way he always did. Or maybe he'd return for a hike to Back Cove again and again, not a trespasser but an observer of the spirit of this place. And maybe, just maybe, something would change for him. And if it can happen to Murray, it can happen to anyone.

Then he turned around again. "By the way, Alana, Ryan here risked his own life out there last winter to save me. He didn't have to but he did. And I never really showed him the proper respect for that. You're both quite courageous. You work well together."

"We know that," Alana said.

"If you two are up for it, maybe we can rent a boat and go out and try to locate my snowmobile. You know, haul it up, get it ashore. It's yours if you want it. You could probably tear the engine down and fix it up."

I just shook my head. "I don't think I'm into ski-doos," I told him.

He threw his hands up in the air. "Ah, what the heck. Maybe we can still rent the boat and I'll take you both out on the harbour. We could just go fishing."

"Maybe," I answered. And he walked away.

Out over the harbour an osprey circled, spiralling upward in a warm wind. And when he saw what he was looking for, he made a fast, hard dive straight down into the water, straight down into the cold, clean water of the harbour.